THE RIOTING OF INFERNO

THE RIOTING OF INFERNO

by

E.J.Cousins

First published in paperback special edition, 2024
By Cybirdy Publishing
101 Camley Street, London N1C 4DU

This book is sold subject to the condition that it shall not, by way of trade,
Digitalisation or otherwise, be lent, resold, hired out or otherwise circulated
Without the publisher's prior consent in any form of binding or cover other
than that in which it is published and without a similar condition being
Imposed on the subsequent purchaser.

Ethan John Cousins, aka E.Jcousins has asserted his rights to be identified
as the author of this work in accordance with the Copyright, Designs and
Patents Act 1988

Cover design by Anwot
Illustrations by Anwot
Printed by Hobbs the Printers Ltd

This book is typeset in Minion, Proxima Nova and Copperplate
A CIP record for this book is available from the British Library

ISBN: 978-1-7396637-8-0

THE RIOTING OF INFERNO

E.J. COUSINS

THE
BIGTIME OF
INFERNO

E.L.COUSINS

HOME IS WHERE THE HELL IS

I can hear it again.

The knocking, the scratching.

It will end tonight. Flinging off the cover, I swung myself out of bed and turned on the light. Kneeling down, I knock on the wood, moving methodically along it until I hear more than a dull thud. It's hollow. Smiling, I move downstairs and brave the cold air, running into my shed and searching through the drawers until I find the hatchet. I dash back inside to the comforting warmth, a grin wrinkling my face.

Returning to my room, I get to work. I hack madly at the wood, splinters flying away from my swings, and efficiently break a panel enough to yank it from the wall. Wincing in pain, I look down at the many splinters that now pepper my hands, and without a pause, I tear them out, dropping each one to the floor and wipe the small droplets of blood on my palm onto the front of my top. Peering inside, I see…. what? No, that's not possible! Now confused, I continue to pull panels from my wall to let more light into the hole. I stand there bewildered as I try and process what I am seeing.

There's a corridor.

I don't move. There's a bathroom on the other side of this wall. How can there be? I hear a knock. I still continue to stare dumbly into the corridor, trying to understand, until another sharp knock echoes out at me, closer this time, pulling me from my confused trance. I now become curious, and going down to my kitchen, I retrieve a torch and, on second thought, a knife. The knocking echoes out of my room. Answering its call, I step into the hole in the wall. I look around my new surroundings, only to find it all to be smooth, dark-grey stone. There is no coating of dust. No cracks, no break in the stone, making it seem like one massive stone. As I move down the corridor, I start to notice that it has become more humid. Beads of sweat are leaking down my forehead, stinging my eyes. My curiosity is quickly stopped as I hear knocking behind me. Whirling round, I look into the darkness, but my light finds nothing. Not even the hole I entered from. Panicking, I run back, but all I find is an endless corridor. Panting, I come to a stop, gasping, begging to see anything but a stone wall.

I scream into the darkness, punching the wall, bloodying my knuckles. My desperate frustration melts into despair, and I slump down, dropping my head between my knees. The silence claws at my head, hungry. The only thing that fends it off is the knocking resuming, only this time, louder. Crawling to my feet, I begin my hunt for the source of the knocking again. Gripping the knife tighter, I plunge into the darkness.

»»»»»»»»

I'm dripping with sweat. The humidity has given way to heat, and becomes so unbearable that I remove my sodden top in a desperate effort to cool down. I stumble forward, swinging the torch weakly. My torch begins to fade, spluttering, clinging to life, until it finally gives in and I'm overcome by the darkness. In alarm, I lunge for a wall, trying to orient myself in the crushing darkness. As my hand hits it, I hear a hiss and crackle and am overwhelmed by the smell of charred meat. In horror, I rip my hand from the wall, leaving my skin burning on its surface. Clutching my raw, bleeding hand, I shriek into the darkness as the heat overwhelms me. The knife clatters to the floor, as I feel my skin start to burn. My scream echoes back at me in reply to the pain. I writhe in the darkness as blisters form across my body, overwhelming me, and I convulse helplessly. The blisters bulge and, one by one, burst. The pus leaks out and slithers down my body, burning me further as it reaches untouched skin. I jerk and thrash on the scalding stone and then—

I hear him.

The darkness twists and burns into me, entering through the open sores that coat my body. It curls and slices through my flesh, pushing against my damaged skin. Hysterically, I tear at myself, desperately trying to exorcise the darkness from my flesh, my head feeling like it will burst, my eyes bulging. My fingers catch on the gaping sores and tear strips of skin and flesh off my body until I'm a bloody, deformed mess. Then, like removing a splinter, the darkness slides from my ravaged flesh.

I am not in control.

It's beautiful. The darkness, pain, my saviour. My agony is what He wants.

I will,

He wants,

I'm helpless, but He …

He gave me the knife, the only way.

He only wants me to see, to understand, to transform.

I can't, won't disappoint him.

I – I must.

I plunge the knife into my face.

I drag it down until it snags and sinks into my eye. I twist, dig, pull. I feel its jelly dribble down my cheek. I drag the knife through my face and hear the crack of bone until the blade finds my other eye and slices gleefully into it. My tears are replaced with the dribbling remains of my eyes. The darkness can now seep into and invade my skull. I drop to my knees, my hands falling to my sides. He's happy.

I smile.

I understand.

It is glorious.

NOT MY SKIN

5th April

You are blind.

But I – I can see who, what, you really are.

You are diseased. Rotting from the inside out. You are lost, with no hope for salvation. The sin has infected every cell in you.

I see so much, so much that you ignore. I've seen people dying, calling out for help, but their cries fall on your broken ears. Alcohol and drugs run rampant in your body, your gift, decimating what He has provided. You will not be saved.

He is coming again, He has sown the seeds for His cleansing, He has created a new race to inherit what He has created. I am His tool, His solution. I have none of the flaws that you do. I feel no pain. I am pure. I can make it through His tests, and I have been given the opportunity to watch you burn and scream for mercy as you are cut, broken, gutted, tortured, until you have been purged from this world. You will inherit nothing.

Those who look down on me for my 'delusions', those who think that they are so much better than me, cannot understand that they are merely shit on my shoe, that they are worth nothing. They must diagnose me with something, CIPA[1], so they can control me, monitor me, force their drugs down my throat, but my faith keeps me safe. They will not veer me from my path of righteousness, my path to salvation. I must complete my metamorphosis.

---

1 Congenital Insensitivity to Pain and Anhidrosis

»»»»»»»»

6th April

It is time for my rebirth.

Stripping naked, I stand in front of the mirror, taking in my imperfect reflection. Steeling myself, I prepare to take my manhood: we will not need it, He will provide. Taking a carving knife, I squeeze my genitals together and pull the blade through them. They drop to the floor as blood begins to spurt out of the wound. Stooping down, I lift my severed genitals to the sky, showing Him that I won't fail my task. I will succeed. Dropping them into the bin, I sit and make an incision around the top of my left thigh and around my knee. I then drag the knife down the inside of my thigh to the cut around my left knee and do the same on the outside. Slipping the knife under my skin, I free it from the muscle. The blood begins to flow more freely and pool at my feet as the knife creates an opening for me to push my fingers under the skin. With enough skin loose to get a firm grip, I slowly peel it off my thigh. Strands of skin stick to the muscle as it is separated off, blood oozing from the exposed flesh. With the top half of my thigh freed, the knife is now able to glide between the muscle and skin on the underside, removing it like skinning a joint of meat. Now that my thigh is complete, I dump the waste into the bin.

The cut around my knee is exposed, with the edge of the skin jutting out against my muscle. Resting the knife on it, I angle the blade inwards and force it down my calf, peeling the skin off like a vegetable. As I move round my leg, the bloody flaps pile around my foot, waiting to be thrown away. Replacing the knife with a peeler, I turn my attention to my foot. Starting on the top, I drag the peeler through my skin, lifting it off the tendons. Once this is finished, my attention is turned to the sides, which only take a couple of attempts to clear. With some persuasion from the knife, I am able to disconnect my sole from its skin. All that is left is to take the peeler to my toes and take off the remaining scraps that had been left untouched. I mirror this on my right leg, with the same success, leaving a pile of discarded gore to be dumped into my bin. I stand in front of the mirror and admire my work so far. He will be proud.

My arms prove to be a bigger challenge, but cleansing my right arm was the easier of the two. With the peeler, I shave my shoulder, and with the knife, I take a strip of skin so I can pull my arm out of it, like taking off a sleeve. Similar to my feet, I am able to clean my fingers with the peeler and take off my palm, which looks amusingly pathetic as it lands on the floor. I am able to shave my other shoulder without too much difficulty, though I drop the peeler partway through. The rest of my arm is a harder challenge. I am able to remove a strip of skin, like I did before, but find that I can't pull it off as easily as I did with my right arm. Out of frustration, I dig my nails into the skin and tear chunks off, tossing them across my room, leaving trails of blood over the floor and walls. Once I have regained control of myself, I remove the rest of the skin, which is much easier now that it is in much smaller patches. Soon, the skin on my hand flops to the floor and joins the diseased gristle.

»»»»»»»»»

I knew that I would not be able to reach all my back alone, so in preparation, I built a tool that would be essential to completing my mission. It is effectively a human-sized grater. I attached two thin metal sheets, which I sharpened, to wooden posts and angled them just enough that the bottom sheet is not under the top piece. The time has now come to see if my hard work will pay off. Propping the grater up against the wall, I press my back to it so the bottom is poking me just above my pelvis and the top is just below my shoulder blades. Now positioned, I let my knees buckle, and I drop to the floor, accompanied by the sounds of tearing skin and a wet slap as my skinless appendages hit the floor. Praying to Him that it worked, I turn my head to see my blood dripping down the blades. Turning to the mirror, I crane my head round to see how much skin is left. Unfortunately, the blades have not cut the skin off, just turned it into skin capes. Huffing with annoyance, I reach around and pull on the skin. It stretches more than I was expecting, and I have to use both arms to tear the skin off, but finally, the hardest part is over and the skin from my back drops into the bin.

I know that my chest will be too big to take off in one piece, so I divide it up into six sections. I make a cut from my collarbone down to my groin and then add horizontal cuts at my belly button, the top of my abs, and then at my collarbone. Now divided, it is easy to slide the knife under the skin, disconnecting as much tissue as possible before tearing it off like a bandage. All that's left now is my neck and head. Picking up a straight razor, I strip down my neck, with bloody clumps sticking to my exposed form. Brushing myself down, I turn to the mirror to shave off my hair.

With my scalp now exposed, I cut an outline of my face, distinguishing it from my scalp. Much like how I shaved the hair, I cut back the scalp, chipping slowly away at it until it is ready to be pulled off like a swimming cap. I just have one more task before I can remove the mask of skin that covers my face. My ears. They catch and hold the inescapable sin that circles me. They cannot be saved, but I don't worry. He does not need sound to talk. It is all part of His plan. My blood rushes in my ears as it pools in the ear canals, muffling the ripping and sawing that the razor creates. I put down the razor, laying it carefully on the floor. In front of the mirror, I closely examine every inch of my new form, scratching and picking off any remains of skin that were not pulled off. When I am sure that I am clean, I lean into the mirror and watch with unbridled joy as I peel off my face. My lips need some help, same with the eyelids, but the peeler takes care of them before they become an issue.

I lift my face to the sky, showing Him my work, my dedication. I pin it to the wall, a symbol of the sin I have defeated, along with the bin full of my skin. Euphoria courses through my form, blurring my sight. I glisten with Holy Glory.

He is coming.

I am here.

CULT OF THE *SANGUINAS CANIS*

"We found it dying. It called to us to restore it. It has been rejected, forgotten by the world, but it will give us power. We have saved it, nursing it back to its rightful place.

"Through many trials, we have found what it needs. The blood of the mother, flesh of the innocent, the sacrifice of the father. We built it a church, a place of safety, a place to feed."

»»»»»»»

The mothers cowered at what I told them. They strained against the ropes and screamed into the gag, unable to understand the purpose their lives had been given. They will help to raise a forgotten god. They cried and begged like they were trying to change my mind.

Sighing, I beckoned in two other men, Isaac and David, and pulling the mothers to their feet by their hair, we dragged them out of their cells and down the tunnel which led to the altar. Walking in, the three women took in the view: the vaulted pillars, the ornate stone carvings on the floor, the worshippers who lined the walls of the circular room. Dropping them at the altar, we cut their ties and stepped back, joining our brothers and sisters. The mothers huddled together on the altar, staring around at us, waiting for their death.

The moment we took our place next to our brothers and sisters, the god lurched out from behind the altar and cracked one of the mother's arms on the stone, revealing broken and bloodied bone. It grabbed the bone, wrenched it from her arm with a wet rip and sunk it through her eye and into her skull. She hung limp in its grasp as it withdrew the bone and placed her head against its featureless face. A horrendous slurping sound filled the space and blood trickled down the god's limbs. Tossing her aside, it turned its attention to the other two mothers. They had tried to escape but were now being held as they thrashed against the wall of worshippers. One of these worshippers, Jacob, held one and pushed her back onto the stone, and the god pounced immediately onto her. Flipping her so she faced it, it tore a hole in her chest, causing her to convulse and spurt blood from her mouth. She could only watch dumbly as the god plunged its head into her chest and began to take her blood. She shook and thrashed and gurgled, but it kept pushing its head further and further into her. Finally, once her efforts had stopped and her final twitches had ceased, the god removed her head, leaving her entrails dangling around its neck like a demented scarf. Shaking them off, it reached for the final mother and, in one clean movement, tore off her head and held her decapitated body over itself, letting the blood drain over its body in a baptism of blood.

The god howled into the sky as the skin on its face was pulled open, creating something resembling a mouth. Nodding to the man next to me, we moved out of the altar room and ascended the tunnel in morbid silence to retrieve the innocents. We found them huddled together in their cell, whimpering for their parents. Leading them by the hand, we shepherded them back down to the god and ushered them towards it. The sight of the gore which decorated the floor made them scream, and one final push forced them to step onto the altar, turning the god's attention away from the corpses and towards the innocents. It surged towards them and instantly dismantled them, abruptly cutting off their screams. It crouched over the pieces, moving them into a pile. From our view, we could make out their heads, a leg, or maybe an arm. That soon changed as black bile started to leak from the god's mouth, landing on the human meat, causing it to smoke. The bile turned it into a putrid-smelling pulp, reminiscent of baby food. Without hesitation, the god began to shovel the slush into its mouth, shoving its whole hand into its face like it was in a rush to consume its meal. We murmured in excitement as we took in the sight. We had not seen the bile before. Last time, the god had dissected the innocents and eaten the pieces whole, seemingly dislocating its jaw to do so. The progress thrilled us and created a sense of impatience. We knew that we were providing what it needed, but it seemed that raising a god would take longer than we had thought.

The god threw itself against a beautifully carved wooden door, which led outside to where the fathers were kept. Its excitement was palpable, and we were not ones to keep a god waiting. We swung open the doors and it followed us outside. In front of us was a wide, expansive field. The night was clear: the moon was unimpeded by clouds and shone onto the field, causing the moisture which clung to the grass to glitter. The light also unveiled what was to come next. There, in the field in front of us, were the three fathers. Each had his own pyre and was bound to it by his ankles, wrists, and neck. As we drew closer, passing old, blackened pyres with crisped bodies and skeletons collapsed in front of them, the fathers started to shout obscenities at us, but quickly fell silent at the sight of the god.

"Beautiful, isn't it?" I told them as the god began to circle the pyres. It taunted them, swiping at their legs, eliciting pained cries from them. Finally, it paused next to the father in the middle and stooped in front of him, signalling its choice. I turned to David, and he handed me a torch and lit it.

The father saw the lit torch, and before he could stop his impudent words, he screamed, "Oh God, please, no!"

"There's no point in begging," I responded, "god wants this."

And with that, I touched the torch to the pyre, and the flames quickly began to lick at the father's feet, teasing him over his fate. The flames leapt up onto his legs, and the sweet smell of cooking meat filled the air. The man's anguished screams rang out, his skin peeled, and the flesh bubbled. Sparks danced in the air until they latched onto his hair. It curled and crisped as the flames engulfed his head, burning through his cheek. A chunk of flesh dropped off his face, exposing his molars. The man's jaw moved up and down in a silent scream as his eyes widened. The fire took the opportunity and darted into his eyes, which released a sizzling sound as they began to melt. They dribbled and boiled out of their sockets and ran down his face. His jaw spasmed and severed his tongue. His clothes had now fused to his torso. The ropes were burning through and finally snapped, allowing the man to collapse into the flames. The deformed shape that was the father dragged himself out of the fire and onto the damp grass. His legs were useless, and the only thing holding them together were the few muscles that hadn't torn. As the man pulled himself towards us, he created a trail of singed dirt. He lay still in front of us, the pungent smell of burnt flesh flooding our senses. He raised his head, with flaps of flesh hanging from his exposed skull. His eyeless face stared at us, seemingly begging for death. We saw that his nose had been completely lost to the fire as his arm reached for us, but we stepped back, out of range from his grasp. The god leapt forward and lopped off the father's head, sending it rolling past our feet. As the head came to a rest, the jaw detached and scattered the teeth out of the bone.

Without thought, the god immediately turned away from the smouldering corpse and selected his next sacrifice. Silently, I retrieved the second torch and moved over to the next father, lighting the pyre. The agonised screams and the delighted howls of the god intertwined and merged as the sound rose into the darkness of the night.

INSECTOIDS

The farmer awoke to the sound of chaos.

The animals were pushing against the barn doors, causing them to bend and groan. The dogs were barking, the horses jumped the fences and galloped into the night. Watching through the window, the famer swore and smacked the glass, rattling the pane, and grabbed his coat as he made his way out of the house and into the sharp cold of the night to pinpoint the source of the panic. Lining the edge of his property was a forest. Out of this forest emanated the glow of a fire, which grabbed the farmer's attention. Content that this is what had startled his animals, the farmer decided to try and find the source of the fire.

The cacophony of his screaming animals dissolved into the night as he dived into the darkness, armed with his torch. His beam of light sliced apart the darkness, searching for the source of the fire, which had now seemingly gone out, but revealing only trees and startled animals. The farmer continued through the trees, the chirping of the birds dying out, the only sound being the soft cracking of twigs under his feet. The light slipped through the trees, revealing a thin but well-worn path. Thankful, the farmer stumbled out of the undergrowth and brushed off the leaves and twigs that clung to his coat and pyjama trousers. He continued his search down the path, becoming aware of a sulphuric stench. The further he walked, the more abrasive and intolerable the smell became. Swinging his torch across the path, he finally spotted a crater just off to the side of the path.

Slicing through the darkness with his torch, he found a black object big enough to carry, sitting in the dirt, seemingly melting into the night. Strange possibilities of the rock-like object quickened his pulse, and he approached, intending to take the rock home. When the farmer got close, though, the object unravelled and revealed itself to be alive. The danger that was twitching in front of him did not stop his approach, and blinded by greed, he continued to creep slowly forward. Once he got close enough, the creature snapped to attention, facing him down. Suddenly hesitant, the farmer tried to back away, but it charged him, leaping towards his face.

The farmer screamed, but the thick body of the creature cut it off as it squirmed into his mouth, trying to force itself down the man's throat. Its legs were like razors and sliced through his flesh with ease, shooting blood down his throat and into his lungs, suffocating him. The farmer stumbled and flailed around the crater, trying to cough out the creature. When this failed, he then wrapped his hands around the creature's torso and began tugging on it, attempting to pull it out of him. These efforts also failed, the creature's legs cutting open his palms and loosening his grip. His hands slid across its body, the blood making it impossible to grip it. The farmer's eyes bulged, and the creature pulled itself further down his throat and finally into his stomach, leaving him spitting out blood.

Gasping, he heard the distant sound of voices and turned with the intent to try and reach them, but the writhing movements in his stomach exploded agony through his body, collapsing him to the ground. Still hoping to reach the voices, he began to drag himself forward, but he quickly passed out, the pain overwhelming him. Inside his stomach, more creatures began to hatch and grow, pushing against his flesh, preparing for birth.

»»»»»»»

"Darling, are you sure this is quicker?"

"Leigh, trust me, it's practically a straight line home. If we cut through the woods, it won't take long."

The husband strode into the woods, leaving his wife staring at the twisted trees in apprehension until, with a deep breath, she moved forward, following her husband. Starting a light jog, she advanced quicker to catch up, struggling to find her husband.

Crack!

She stopped dead in her tracks. Slowly turning around, she squinted into the darkness behind her, trying to find the source of the noise. Going closer to where she heard it, the sound of ragged breathing became audible. Her stomach contorted as the breathing became louder and closer.

"Hello?" she ventured nervously.

A figure leapt from the darkness, tackling her to the ground. Screaming, she tried to drag herself up until he began laughing. As she turned around, her fear melted into anger.

"James, you dick!"

"Oh, lighten up! What's the worst thing out here? A stray dog? Ooh, maybe a bear?!"

Thoroughly annoyed, the wife just sighed and asked, "Can we just keep moving? Please?"

Chuckling to himself, the husband continued with his wife in tow. Apart from the occasional mutterings from the wife, their journey through the woods was silent. That was until they found the bloated man. He was lying in a hole to the side of the path, curled into a ball. Concerned he was hurt, the husband rushed down and rolled him onto his back.

Immediately, it was clear that something was wrong. The man's stomach was swollen, or more accurately, looked inflated, like it had been pumped full of air. Pushing the man's t-shirt up, the husband began to probe his stomach, searching for any cause of the inflation. Suddenly, something writhed and rippled under the man's skin, causing the husband to launch himself backwards. The bloated man's eyes flew open as a twisted scream pushed itself out of his mouth. He crawled up onto the path and rolled onto his back, unable to stand up.

"In … side … Get out!"

Before the husband could say anything, the man convulsed, and his chest and abdomen burst open. As his back arched, darkness spilled out from the hole, flooding towards the couple. Pushing his wife back, the husband was overrun, and in the moonlight, the wife realised her husband's face was being eaten. She was able to see that the darkness was a swarm of insect-like creatures, creatures so black they melted into the night. She watched as their legs sliced easily through her husband's flesh, exposing bone and teeth as they curled over his face. One insectoid dropped to the floor, squirming on its back until it could right itself. In those moments, the wife was able to see that the thing's entire underside was composed solely of thin, curved teeth. Shuddering with horror, she stumbled back as her husband twitched to his feet, his face now replaced with the writhing body of one of the insectoids. Sobbing, the wife turned and fled, praying that she could find her way back to the town. Hungry, the insectoids followed.

》》》》》》》》

Entering the town square, the wife spun around, seeking any signs of life. She finally caught sight of a restaurant that was still open and, gasping with relief, burst in. The occupants turned to her, watching curiously as the wife leant on the door, panting.

"They're coming! We, we need to run!" was all the wife could muster before she slumped down against the door. A man approached and stood her up, walking her further into the dining area. The woman stood petrified in the centre of the restaurant as the man tried to comfort her.

"Who is coming?" he asked slowly, hoping to find out what had panicked her.

"The things, they, they…" she trailed off and began to sob again, leaving the diners in the dark as to what was rapidly approaching them. Shrugging off offers of water and ignoring the staff, the wife continued into the back of the restaurant, wailing about the killing of her husband and strange creatures made of darkness, leaving the customers to their fate as the door burst open.

There was no screaming.

The insectoids leapt into the mouths of those trying to scream, breaking through their hard palates, and slithering in and out of their eyes, feasting until all that was left was the insectoid, now in control. The husband staggered into the restaurant and grabbed hold of a woman who was trying to escape the massacre and drove his fingers into her eyes. She shrieked as the blood flowed down her cheeks. The husband then shoved his thumb through the roof of the woman's mouth and tore off the front of her skull, letting her drop to the floor. Immediately, the insectoids swarmed over the corpse, invading the exposed brain until the body came shuddering back to life.

One man held out his hand, trying to fend off a creature, but it chewed through his palm and slid under his skin, moving up his arm, and finally burst out into the man's mouth. Gurgling, he fell too. Bodies littered the floor, strips of flesh missing. Bodies convulsed and clawed themselves. Bodies became vessels.

The corpses marched into the kitchen and were met with a collection of knives and cleavers. The chefs cowered away from the horde, swinging wildly at their outstretched arms. Occasionally, a cook would lop a finger off or catch a wrist, making the hand hang from the arm by the remaining skin. This proved ultimately pointless, as when a body became too damaged, the insectoid would leap out of its corpse and take over the cook. The wife had taken this opportunity to escape into the alley behind the restaurant, but it didn't take long for her to be followed. She was thrown against a wall and the convulsing corpse of her husband forced its fingers into her mouth and pulled it open, her tongue flapping in a choked scream. Leaning over her, the insectoid released a stream of pellets down her gullet. It let go, and she immediately retched, trying to purge herself of the pellets. She was left slumped against a wall in the alleyway, waiting for the inevitable. It started quickly with a cramping sensation but rapidly turned to burning as she watched her stomach expand. Screaming into the air, she suffered as the creatures consumed her from the inside out. Bruising started to form across her chest until, finally, the tips of the insectoids' legs began to protrude from her flesh. Like a dam breaking, her chest tore open, and the creatures poured out, spilling into the alley. This was the last thing that the wife saw before death took her. The sight of the insectoids pouring out of her chest cavity, pulling scraps of her organs with them, slowly faded as her body gave in.

The insectoids filled the town, spilling into every street, every home, every head. Soon, the town could not hold them. Soon, nothing would.

RESOLUTION

The damaged, stained, and worn pages floated to the ground, a sign that The Writer's goal was finally completed. Sighing, The Writer slumped back into his chair.

»»»»»»»

Time did not exist within The Writer's study. There was only a dark-brown cabinet, an oak desk, and an ancient chair with padding and a leather cover. The walls consisted of a composite wood panelling and a beige carpet. There was no clock in the room to limit distractions and extra noises, and there was only the one lamp hanging over the desk, casting a dim, orange light into the room. The desk was covered with scattered piles of paper with a pot of black pens next to it, and on a coaster sat a sticky and stained tumbler glass half-filled with whisky. In the chair sat The Writer.

He sat on the edge of the chair, bent over a piece of paper, scribbling manically. He had been there for days, but the only thing in his mind was the need to finish the work. Fuelled by alcohol and the obligation to finish the rites, he was only interrupted by his hand cramping. Over time, he became infuriated by how inefficient this was becoming. So, the next time his hand cramped, he ignored it and continued to write. The hand shook, and the pen clattered onto the desk. Screaming and pounding the arms of his chair, The Writer climbed to his feet and strode to the cabinet to his right. Tearing open the drawers, he ripped through the contents until he found a roll of packing tape.

Grabbing the tape and the pen, he pulled on the end and began to wrap his hand with it, stopping only when the hand was covered, then retook his seat and restarted his work. The pen did not move, and when the fingers cramped, The Writer was able to continue. Pages and pages were completed, covered with rites and diagrams. The pile of pages grew, and the packing tape seemed to work. A hungry grin stretched across his pale face as he charged through the work. Then his hand began to sweat, and the adhesive loosened and began to stick to the paper. The pen was beginning to slip.

Shouting in frustration, The Writer grabbed an envelope opener and stabbed it into the tape. He began to saw at it, and a mixture of blood and sweat started to leak out. Undeterred, he continued until the pen had been freed. Deep tears and rips were visible on his hand, but The Writer ignored the injuries. Resuming, he quickly knew that without the tape, he would not be able to continue writing for long. Snapping his head around, he scanned the study until his eyes settled on a sewing kit. Leaping over, he grabbed a roll of string and a handful of needles, many piercing his hand. Collapsing back down into the desk chair, he picked up the tumbler glass and drained the contents. Using the now-empty glass and a needle, he slammed the glass down onto the head of the needle, punching holes into the pen. When one edge of the pen was littered with holes, he frantically threaded the string through the needle. Filling up the tumbler glass once more and drinking most of it, he pushed the needle through the top of the index finger, then through the first hole in the pen, then back into the finger, blood creeping out of the needle holes. Now switching to sew the thumb to the pen, he continued working down until he reached the end of the pen. Pulling the string as hard as possible, he tightened it until the index finger and thumb could not move and were fastened to the pen.

Putting the pen to paper, The Writer continued his task. The pile of pages grew, and the pile of clean paper shrank. His fingers were numb, his jaw clenched, the pen creaking. Finally, under the pressure, the pen began to crack. Panicking, The Writer began to work faster, his other hand feeding the tumbler with alcohol. Eyelids heavy, hand screaming in pain, he pulled out an EpiPen and thrust it into his thigh, adrenaline forcing his body awake. The string was fraying, the pen cracking, the pages getting torn and creased. The cracks overcame the pen, which finally relented and broke.

Heart racing, and without much thought, The Writer grabbed the remains of the pen and ripped it from his hand. Skin was flapping, flesh exposed, and blood was flowing. Grabbing tissues, he stuffed them into the wounds, absorbing the blood. Knocking over the pot of pens, he scrambled for a new tool. Knowing his hand could not hold a pen now, he scoured drawers and cupboards and snatched a tube of super-glue. Biting off the cap, he squeezed the glue onto the mangled hand and pen, and it hardened, making hand and pen one. Laughing, The Writer started the last leg of his work. Finished pages were being thrown off the desk: the expectation of completion grew and clawed around inside him. Breathing heavily, his body was shaking: the end was teasing him. Lungs gasping, hand dying, heart weakening. More alcohol was consumed. His hand was failing, but The Writer forced it to move. The final pieces of paper were covered in illegible writing.

The damaged, stained, and worn pages floated to the ground, a sign of The Writer's goal finally being completed. Sighing, The Writer slumped back into his chair. His hand hung limp over the arm of the chair, a rock of glue holding his hand and the pen together. His mouth hung open and his heart faltered. His work was finished, but at the greatest cost.

»»»»»»»

The Writer released a soul-shuddering sigh, and with a glass of whisky in one hand and a glue-covered pen in the other, The Writer felt complete, whole.

A resolution had been reached.

FAVOUR

The eyes, the – why they are so black, no, empty? How are they hollow that, I didn't mean to hurt him.

His tears are **wrong**,
> so wrong they're red, are red. Why is he crying? he wanted my help, my help, but he lies to me, he wanted my help, he wanted, now I'm stained, he made me red, I'm not red, his bones, they are red he is red he is infecting me. He tried, wanted to …

punish

> me, why he wanted, he thought **I** was **evil**, I'm good, GOOD, I was freeing it is evil, cracked his mind like an egg.
> I would be quick, his life would be gone, on the floor, but he wanted it to hurt, made it hurt, why? He wanted,
> asked me to free him, so he made it hurt,
> wanted the pain, but no one wants pain,
> devils make pain he was **devil**,
> daemon wanted pain, I killed him, it, he asked me for it.

> His stupidity made it hard he is everywhere, the wall floor me his blood is on my mouth, made a mess, how will I clean it? I won't, it was his fault, I don't make a mess, it's quick and easy, but he threw bits of him everywhere. The saying, guts for garters, did I garter him, his guts are in the wrong place now, I did then, they left his corpse joined me, **me**.

Why did he do it, he lied, why?

>   nononono

 I KILLed the man, he made it hard, I'm red, shouldn't be red, he is red I made him **red**, he is where he should be, not here gone.

Gone

THE CRYING

"Congratulations, it's a boy!"

Smiling weakly, The Mother reached out longingly for her child, watching lovingly as he was lowered into her arms. She fell asleep with the child wrapped in her warmth; their breathing synchronised as they drifted away from consciousness.

She awoke the next morning alone. She immediately started to look around the room, searching for her child. The walls were off-white and undecorated, with the fluorescent lights emitting a dirty, yellow light. In front of her bed were two windows, but these were covered with blinds, isolating her from the outside world. All she could hear was the buzzing of the lights and the distant beeping of machines.

Ringing for a nurse, she asked, panicked: "Where's my baby?" She was reassured that he had been taken for a routine check-up and that nothing was wrong. Relieved, The Mother sunk back down into her bed, wiping her hair from her eyes.

"Did the father join us?" inquired the nurse, but The Mother replied in the negative, explaining that he was not in the picture. Nodding understandingly, the nurse finished her checks of The Mother's vitals and left her alone once more. Closing her eyes, The Mother began to fall into sleep again, but was quickly jolted awake by the entrance of a doctor.

"As you may well know–," started the doctor, but he was interrupted by The Mother.

"Where is my baby? A nurse told me that he was getting checked, but where exactly is he?"

Sighing slightly, the doctor tried to calm the woman down. "He is a few floors down, getting checked. If you agree to what I am trying to offer you, then you will be taken to him. If you don't, then he will be brought back up to the maternity ward."

The Mother nodded, but her brow stayed knotted in concern. The doctor took no notice and moved back to the reason for his visit.

"As you may well know, we usually recommend the first round of vaccinations to come at 8 weeks of age for the child, but, free of extra charge, there is a vaccine being tested at the moment which potentially would erase the need for further vaccinations. A life-long vaccine, so to speak. It has just entered the first stage of human trials, and you would be one of the first in it.

"The only thing that we ask of you is that you stay in the accommodation provided by us so that we can monitor the both of you. You would be comfortable, food would be provided, and you would be in an apartment-like setting. On top of this, if you complete the trial, a small percentage of your hospital bill will be taken off as a show of gratitude."

"How much is a small percentage?"

"Depending on the period of time you spend in the trial, anywhere from 10 to 20% could be taken off."

"And it won't hurt my baby?"

"There has been no sign that it will hurt any babies."

"When would it start?"

"We could begin straight away; you would just need to sign a consent form."

Pulling a form out, he handed it over to The Mother, who, after a pause, signed it. The doctor helped The Mother out of her bed and led her towards the elevator. The corridor matched her room. The walls were plain, the floor was formed of dirty white tiles smeared with old, dried blood, and the lights continued to buzz. As The Mother walked, the continuous buzzing started to drill into her, and she raised a hand to her head, aware of a headache forming. Entering the elevator, The Mother had to squint as it contained a harsh, bright light. The doctor pressed the bottom button, and the elevator shuddered to life, and it began to drop, trembling, down to the basement.

"Why are we going to the basement?" The Mother probed, confused as to why her child would be there.

"All experimental trials are placed in the basement. There's really nothing to worry about," said the doctor, brushing her off and returning the journey down to silence.

Banging to a halt, the elevator doors screeched open, revealing another identical corridor. Stepping out, The Mother shuddered from the cold and again followed the doctor to another side room. Sitting her down, the doctor left to get her child, and The Mother sat alone, looking at the dust-coated inspection bed and the scratched, wooden desk that sat opposite the door. The door swung open again, the doctor returning with her baby in his arms, and dropping him into her lap, he sat down and pulled out the vaccine.

"Due to the size of it, I will administer it through two injections. The first will be at the base of the child's skull, and the second on the upper arm, like your usual injection."

Turning the child's head, the doctor injected the first half of the vaccine. The child squirmed in The Mother's grasp, the needle causing him obvious discomfort. The doctor wasted no time in following this up with the final injection and was soon taking the child's heartbeat, blood pressure, and temperature to log the child's reaction to the vaccine.

"Everything is looking good so far. If you wait here, I'll fetch a pair of doctors who are also part of the vaccine trial to take you to your accommodation."

Watching the doctor leave, The Mother turned her attention to comforting the child, who was still crying after the injections. Rocking him finally to sleep, she admired her baby, not seeing the slight swelling around the injection sites.

»»»»»»»»

It won't stop.

I've fed it, changed its fucking diaper, but it won't stop crying.

It won't let me sleep. Anytime it shuts up, and I try and close my eyes, it starts again. I can't remember the last time I slept; days and nights have blended, and I'm starting to forget the most normal things. I can't remember if I've eaten, I don't even think I've changed my clothes recently. Well, then again, who will see me? I can't leave this apartment; I'm stuck constantly trying to shut the child up. I have tried everything, every type of earplug, noise-cancelling headphones, but the cries still burrow into my skull. The thin walls vibrate with the pointless cries of the child, invading me when I try to finally sleep.

I've tried to block the noise from the source. Hanging towels over the door doesn't work; it comes through the walls. I've gagged it, but it just takes the gag off. Somehow the thing managed to take off fucking duct tape. It lives to torment me. Sleeping pills can't protect me from this child. It keeps me up, burning through the meds, depriving me of sleep. I feel like I'm withering away, being sapped of life by my own child. I can't leave the apartment; it's trapped me in, blocking the doors with its cries. There's only one way left to fix this.

I can't think about it, only do it. I'll be hated, but sleep, I need sleep. There is no alternative. Walking into its room, I watch its movements, hating every twitch it produces. I'm surrounded by cold blue walls, toys scattered over the carpeted floor. Lifting a pillow over the crib, I press it over the thing's head, muffling the noise. Its movements become frantic, trying to escape, but if it won't let me escape, then I won't let it. Finally, its limbs grow still, and the screeching trails off. Sighing with relief, overwhelmed by the silence, I sink sobbing into my bed, and my eyes drift closed as sleep finally graces me.

»»»»»»»

It's crying again.

It won't shut up. It's stabbing, breaking through my head, gripping me, echoing in my skull. Screaming, I hammer my head into the wall, leaving a bloody stain as my wails match its own. Tears leak from my eyes, mixing with my blood, and I collapse, defeated. Stumbling into the kitchen, I pick up a knife and, without a moment's thought, drive it through both of my ears, relief slowly seeping into me as its cries are muted and replaced with the rushing sound of my blood.

Breathing deeply, I relish this new sound, thankful it isn't the child. Sitting on the tiled floor of the kitchen, I let my head rest on the cupboard behind me, blood staining my top in two parallel streaks of red. But somehow, some-fucking-how, the crying oozes into my broken ears. Laughing hysterically at this incomprehensible feat, I march into the child's room once more and sink the knife into its head. That unequivocally silenced the screaming. It can't come back, not again, let me sleep, I can now sleep. The bed pulls me in and lets me luxuriate in the peace. This time, I will sleep. With open arms and closed eyes, I let sleep embrace me.

》》》》》》》

I can hear it.

THE SURGEON

Wading through my mail, an unusually bright envelope catches my eye. Tearing it open, I examine the ticket that is inside. It is inscribed with the text:

Congratulations! You are the lucky winner of the 2023 Fitness Random Draw Competition! You have won a free trial of our new spa facilities! See the back for more details.

Creasing my brow in confusion, I turn the ticket over and over in my hands, trying to remember if I had entered myself into the competition. Looking at it in more detail, I find instructions on the back, and after a closer inspection, I realise that it holds details on how to redeem my prize and the address for the spa. Over the course of the evening, I think about the ticket and begin to believe that I had been given it by accident. If that was the case, and it wasn't meant for me, then surely there wouldn't be any harm in taking advantage of the opportunity? My mind made up, I set out the next evening in search of the spa.

I drive out of the city and find the spa on its outskirts. It stands alone, surrounded by empty, boarded-up buildings, some with scaffolding, some clearly rotting. The spa itself stands like a beacon, the only source of light in sight. I start to become uneasy, believing that I misread the address. Reading it again, I shake off my unease and make my way across the derelict street and into the building.

Approaching the woman at the front desk, I ask about the competition. Glancing up at me, seemingly annoyed by my question, she reassures me that I am, in fact, the intended recipient of the ticket and that my name was in their database. I start to ask about the competition, but before I can, I am ushered into a side room, which I assume by appearance to be a doctor's office. The doctor in the room turns and greets me, saying:

"Ah, the man of the hour! I was hoping that you would accept our invitation!"

"Uh, yeah, nice to meet you," I reply tentatively, as the doctor vigorously shakes my hand.

"So, what have I won exactly?"

"Well, first, I will do a full medical check-up to make sure you are a prime specimen of man, then I will show you to your first treatment."

"Specimen?"

"Ah, sorry, a turn of phrase that I used back in my old career. I used to work in a laboratory, you see."

Humouring the doctor, I just nod and sit down. The next half an hour is spent with the doctor taking blood, testing my lung capacity, strength, and asking for a detailed account of my exercise and dietary routines. The constant peppering of questions make my head spin. Just when I think he's done, he opens a drawer, revealing a pile of puzzles. I am then made to solve them, and finally, the exam ends with an eye test.

Throughout this, the doctor scribbles down extensive notes and adds the results to a spreadsheet, comparing me to other results. Suddenly, he claps, spinning to face me, a wide grin spreading across his face.

"It is as we had hoped! You are just who we thought you would be. It's very exciting. Don't worry! You are in prime health to try the new treatment that we have recently created. By the end, I guarantee that you will be a new man. But first, as we get everything ready for you, we will give you the chance to unwind and relax, a bit of R&R, in our sensory deprivation tank."

Leading me by the arm, he shows me to the changing rooms. I get changed and he places me hurriedly into one of the tanks.

"See you soon," the doctor whispers with a wink before closing

THE SURGEON

the lid and leaving me in darkness. Closing my eyes and allowing myself to relax, I fail to notice the gas that has begun to creep into the tank, and without realising it, I slip out of consciousness.

»»»»»»»»

Clawing my way back to consciousness, I am met with the voice of The Surgeon.

"You're a fine specimen, fine specimen indeed. It's only courteous now that you are momentarily back with the living to inform you of what is about to happen. I am going to be harvesting your organs, eyes, and brain. The reason why is none of your concern though. You won't be around to admire the finished piece."

Shit, I can't move. Why can't I move? Why won't my eyes close?

"By the erratic movements of your eyes, I can tell you've realised your state of limited mobility. I have paralysed you with my brilliant mix of Belladonna and Hemlock, both lovely neuromuscular toxins. Furthermore, I have pinned your eyes open to make sure you stay conscious, of course. Wouldn't want you to die prematurely and miss out on all the fun!"

No, no, no, no! What the fuck, why me? Who is he? Oh God, please help me, help me!

"You can also put your mind to rest. I've numbed you, so you shouldn't feel any pain. I'm not sadistic, you know. Pain, you see, is an ugly contaminant - really messes up your bits and pieces. Anyway, enough chat, I should begin. Wouldn't want the numbing agent to wear off halfway through, would we?"

With a wicked grin, he pulls a surgical mask over his mouth and slides his hands into a pair of gloves. Picking up a scalpel, he cuts me open from the collarbone to my groin.

"Wow, your heart looks like it'll break through your ribcage for me!"

The Surgeon replaces the scalpel with what appears to be bolt cutters and methodically works his way round my ribs until he lifts them out before my eyes. Returning to the scalpel, he begins to remove my organs.

He isn't lying; I cannot feel any pain, but that doesn't mean I can't feel anything. I am aware of his hands plunging into my chest and exploring his options. He chooses my kidneys first. I stare at the ceiling as I experience him pulling them up and over my intestines, and I feel the tug of his scalpel as he cuts them loose and the smell of burning as he cauterises the wounds.

Showing them to me, he compliments me on their condition before placing them outside my field of view. Next, he unravels my intestine, piling it under my chin. With a resounding, "Ah, there it is!" he detaches the small intestine from the large, the muffled feeling of his scalpel glancing through my guts. Dragging them off my chest, he directs them into what sounds like a tub.

I think I'm going to be sick.

The reality of my situation finally sinks in, and with that comes nausea. As my throat begins to convulse, The Surgeon takes notice and quickly moves to remove my stomach.

"No, no, no! We can't have you dirtying up yourself now, can we?"

Stringing it out like a wet sock, he places my stomach amongst my other pieces. I can feel his hands as they explore my liver, looking for my pancreas. Finally, he finds it and, with a dull tearing sensation, relieves me of it and presents it to me before placing it to one side. I suddenly start to feel a tightness in my chest, and hope bubbles up that this signals my death. Unfortunately, my hopes are soon killed by The Surgeon remarking, "Sorry about that. Just had to move your heart out of the way to extract your liver."

Shit.

"Now, I will warn you that I must make a slight modification to the schedule. I have tried before to implement a combination of artificial lungs and heart, with little success. Due to this, I will only be removing your heart and replacing it with a pump before taking your eyes and prepping your head for the removal of your brain. After that, though, I will take your lungs like I said and quickly move on to your brain. Just thought I should keep you up to date."

With that The Surgeon rolled in a large machine with translucent tubes extruding from the sides, and left it next to me. With concerning speed, my heart is detached in his hand as he pushes the tubes into my chest. We both watch as my blood spurts into it, travelling to the machine, which then returns the blood to my body. With a nod of satisfaction, he steps forward, next to my head. Revealing a pair of tweezers, he leans forward as I try and fail to close my eyes. My vision blurs and distorts as the tweezers squeeze my eye, and suddenly half my vision disappears. Without skipping a beat, The Surgeon ends my sight. I sink into the darkness, now only accompanied by the muffled sensations of The Surgeon's work and my thoughts. Despair darkens my surroundings as, finally, I give up. I don't flinch when I am scalped, or when I hear the sound of a drill hitting bone.

"We're almost done now. You've done so well. Thank you for your donations."

Now the door of death has opened. He disconnects my lungs, and my throat convulses, begging for oxygen. My suffocating is thankfully cut short as my brain is removed from its shell and is decisively cut from the stem.

With relief, I walk through the door of Death.

SECRETS

My father said, "Curiosity killed the cat."
God, how I wished I had listened.

»»»»»»»

My mother died when I was young. I lived alone with my father in an old, decrepit cottage in the centre of the woods, devoid of life. The gnarled trees twisted and contorted around our home, creating a natural wall. My father had his secrets, it was only natural. He would arrive home late, maybe around one or two in the morning, but he worked, had a job, so I didn't think anything of it.

That changed one night. Rain was throwing itself against my window; the shrill cry of the wind rang out through the woods, and flashes of lightning tore open the sky, throwing distorted shadows across my walls. I was lying in bed staring at the beams on the ceiling when my father arrived home. I only took notice when I heard him dragging a heavy object up the stairs.

Thump.
Pause.
Thump.

This continued until I heard him reach the summit of the stairs. It was then that I heard him dragging a heavy plastic bag around to his room. Confused, I rolled over and managed to drift off to sleep.

»»»»»»»

The next morning, I said nothing of the previous night and made my way to school, trudging through the dead woods. Over the course of the day I began to wonder if this had happened before. So, that night, I crept my way to the kitchen and started to make coffee. I had little experience with being awake in the early hours of the morning, so I was fully reliant on caffeine to keep me vigilant. The aroma of the coffee wafted up and slid into my head to smack my brain awake. With caffeine preventing me from falling asleep, I washed the mug and replaced it, determined to keep this secret from my father.

Suddenly, hearing the key scratch the inside of the lock, my heart surged into my mouth and sent me scrambling up the stairs to hide in my bed. Not soon after I had made my retreat, I heard the *Thump*. Pause. *Thump*. Pause. Then, my father reached the top of the stairs, but this time I heard an extra *thump*. Turning over to stare at the wall, I concentrated on keeping every muscle I could control still, attempting to slow my heart and regulate my breathing. His footsteps approached. He was outside my door. The hinges squealed and the door opened. With wide eyes, I saw the light grow on my wall, a warm, golden streak, quickly infected by the bottomless black shadow of my father looming and towering over my still form. It stayed for what could have been seconds, minutes, hours, but in that moment, time had removed itself from that room. He started into my bedroom, but a plastic rustling drew his attention away from me. The looming silhouette retreated, the golden light reclaiming its space before the door was closed and the light was severed.

Thump.

》》》》》》》》》》

Holding my breath, I snuck down the stairs, cursing the morning light for giving my shadow weight. The only thing on my mind was how much I needed to get out. Down the stairs. Bag over my shoulder. Door beckoning me closer. My father, blocking the way.

We stared at each other, waiting to see who would make the first move.

Taking a slow breath, my father said, "Were you in the kitchen last night?"

"No." My heart sped up.

"There was a spoon with coffee stains on the counter. It was still damp."

Clenching my teeth, I replied, "I–I couldn't sleep."

"You couldn't sleep, so you had coffee?" my father replied, his voice laced with sarcasm.

I took this moment of bafflement to slip past him and gratefully met the cold, crisp morning air, still feeling the burning gaze of my father focused on me until I had vanished into the woods.

»»»»»»»

That night, my curiosity over my father's nocturnal hobbies had taken over me, my common sense restrained in the furthest corners of my mind, as I decided to investigate his room. This would be the first place to search, I thought, due to hearing my father walk up to his room most nights, dragging the mystery object behind him. So, when I heard the front door close and his footsteps dissipate into the night, I made my way into my father's bedroom.

It consisted of a single bed with plain brown sheets, pulled taut over the mattress, not a crease in sight. An old oak wardrobe and a rickety bedside table, which held a lamp, and an alarm clock filled the rest of the room. Sifting through the drawers, I could only find underwear and socks, neatly folded and organised, and boxes of tissues. The only thing that caught my attention was a packet of disinfectant wipes along with disinfectant spray that resided in the bottom drawer. Moving on, I opened his wardrobe, finding my father's range of plain, and in some cases, moth-eaten clothes. With drawers and wardrobes searched, I took a step back to try and find any other places to search. I thought about looking through my father's office, which was downstairs, but I ruled it out, having heard my father dragging things up the stairs at night. Trying to focus my eyes, I settled on the hidden void under the bed. Lying down on the cold, hardwood floor, I stretched my arm into the unknown. Sliding my am around, my fingers found plastic. Grabbing it between two fingers, I pulled it into the light.

It was a shoebox in a sealed, transparent plastic bag.

Breaking the seal, I removed the shoebox. I was punched with the stench of rotting meat, which made me drop the box and caused my eyes to start watering. Covering my nose, I slowly opened it, my father's words ringing in my ears. What I saw burned and clawed itself into my memory. It was full of fingers. Some bone picked clean by time, some rotting, oozing pus and tinged green, some fresh, speckled with blood. Some with rings, some without. Some male, some female. Horrified, I leapt away from it, disgust pouring through my body.

"What did I tell you about curiosity, son?"

Spinning, I was terrified to see my father standing in the doorway, body bag behind him with a hand hanging limply out of the zip. I froze. I could not move, speak, or even flinch when he started to advance towards me.

"You're ready," were the only words he spoke before pulling open a hatch that I didn't know existed, leading into an attic I didn't know we had. "Climb."

I stared up at its gaping mouth, and stuttering, prodded by my father's repeated command, I rose, rung by rung, until it devoured me. An old lightbulb blinked into life, unveiling the horrors of my father's life. Bodies swung, creaking, forever silent from the beams, wrapped in horrific plastic cocoons, my father an endless void behind me.

"Wh–what ...?" was the only sound that made it beyond my lips.

"They are not here for long, don't worry. They just stay here before I get rid of them," he said casually. "Oh! Since this will be your first time, I will let you use my knife. Obviously, you will get your own soon, but for now, you can use mine."

I turned to face him and looked at the outstretched hilt, then the

grin which had curled across his face. Like I was in a stupor, my hand grasped the hilt and moved to face a hanging body. Grabbing its hand, I raised it and brought the blade to the skin.

"Now remember, back and forth, let the blade do the work."

Jaw clenched, I began. It slipped through the skin and flesh of the hand, hitting the bone almost immediately. Like I was cutting wood, I started to saw back and forth, back, and forth. I suddenly regained my senses and realised what was happening. I looked down to see blood oozing onto my hand, slinking down my forearm, and, repulsed by what I was doing, I staggered back.

"Come on, you're halfway there!" my father complained, but I was not listening. I was facing him again, shaking my head over and over, blade pointed toward him. Grabbing my hand in an iron grasp, he started to turn me back to the body. Refusing to continue, I stood my ground. "Don't be like your mother!" he grunted, infuriated by my refusal of his orders, the knife trembling in both our grasps.

Words caught in my throat, I lunged forward, catching my father off guard. His back slammed into the low roof, his elbows buckling, and the blade slid gleefully into his chest. Gasping, he looked at me, betrayal filling his eyes. Filled with emotion and adrenaline, I twisted the blade and dragged it down his torso. As his chest opened, he began to fall forward like a felled tree. We came crashing down together, his guts spilling out onto me, piling up on both sides of us. After I regained my breath, I rolled my father off me. We lay there, father and son, as my father bled to death. I looked over, seeing blood spurt rhythmically out of the hole I had made, watching it start to slow down, then trickle, until he lay still. Killed by his son, using his blade. I lay there in silence, horrified at the irony that my father had crafted everything that would lead to his passing. I laughed, I thought, maybe not even laughter. My chest heaved, tears fell from my eyes, somewhere between laughing and crying. My only company was my father's words ringing and echoing in my head: "Remember, son, curiosity killed the cat."

WARM EMBRACE OF DEATH

Darkness painted the corners of the world, watching each of us, waiting until it was allowed to take us. Unbeknownst to the woman who was walking through a picturesque side alley with high, cut-brick arches, sloped, tiled roofs, and vines adorning the walls, her time was up. Her last sights would be these structures and age-stained brick, not her family or husband, but these emotionless walls who would not talk of her end. Even the sun looked away, covered by clouds, withholding its warmth and lengthening the shadows.

The Hag found her and seeped out of the darkness. The further it emerged into the light, the more a distinct shape began to form. Arrows of light which pierced the shadow became holes in its robe, exposing the ragged and worn nature of the being. The slices of robe fell, slinking to the cobbled stone, snaking out behind it silently. Long, rotting arms reached out for the woman from its darkness, skin hanging loose on its bones. Wart-adorned fingers with dirty and broken nails unfurled, grasping at the woman.

The arms finally reached their target. One stretched over the woman's shoulder, coming to rest with its hand curled across her throat, the other twisted around her waist, and together, they drew her unwillingly into the folds of its robes. The woman tugged and pulled against the force as she tried to scream, but terror paralysed her voice. As the torn darkness dropped over her shoulders and brushed against her sides, she gradually began to relax in its arms, her attempts to scream becoming less forceful, until her mouth closed, eternally silent. A warmth had spread through her, comforting her in these pivotal moments.

Now, a head pushed its way to the light, revealing a lipless mouth and a pair of deep, cataract-set eyes matched with a missing nose. Its teeth caressed the woman's neck before its jaw clenched and sank into her flesh. Her life drained and dripped down her white dress, but she felt no pain. The blood splattered on the stone, quietly dripping down. Her right arm reached up, and her fingers slid in between The Hag's fingers, clenching her neck in a display of reassurance. Once the flow of blood had ceased, she fell limp in its arms, mouth hanging silently open, eyes half closed. Slowly, The Hag drew her into its darkness, removing her from this world. The Hag, now alone, sank back into the shadows, dissolving out of existence once again.

It was now waiting, waiting for its time once more.

It would not need to wait long.

THE HUSK

As the storm settled over the mountain, a group of five hikers searched desperately for anything to provide respite from the rain. One of them spotted a cave, and after calling out to the others, they gratefully entered, sighing as the rain ceased to pummel their shoulders.

They noticed that the cave extended into the mountain, and curious, they decided to explore. After a few minutes, they entered a cavern, and in the centre sat a shrine. The shrine consisted of a circle of skulls, yellowed and cracked by age, accompanied by groupings of long, cold, and melted candles. In the centre sat a husk, pale and lifeless. It was bald, with deep gaping holes having long replaced its eyes. Its jaw looked dislocated, jutting out at an unnatural angle, with torn lips and toothless gums. The fingers had scratched through its cheeks and rested in its mouth. The forearms had been tied together by thick string, which had been looped through its flesh. It epitomised agony.

Unnerved, the group turned to leave but were horrified when they found no exit to the cavern. Their torches failed and cut out, leaving them stranded in darkness. An ear-piercing scream echoed out, rebounding off the walls and sending them crashing to their knees, pushing their hands to their ears in an attempt to block out the screaming.

Despite his efforts, the ears of one of the hikers, Glen, a thin man, had started to bleed. Unbeknown to the others, he had dropped his hands to his sides and let the screaming envelop him. He lifted his head and smiled into the darkness. Finally, the hikers' torches came on again, and the screaming stopped, allowing them to regain their senses. Moaning in pain, they clambered to their feet and moved quickly away from the husk. Panic gripped them as they scanned the walls for any sign of an exit. Eventually, they noticed that one among them was smiling.

Turning on Glen, they began to throw accusations at him, blaming him for the noise, the lack of exits, even the shrine at the centre of the cave. The only thing that broke the hikers' shouting was the crack of a rock breaking through the skull of Charlie, Glen's brother. Glen, with his ears still bleeding, had stuck a jagged piece of stone through his brother's skull, exposing his brain to the sharp, cold air of the cave. The other three men stood motionless as they stared at the corpse, trying to process the attack. Without warning, one of them, Chris, a stocky man, returned the hit and knocked out Glen's teeth with the rock, leaving his jaw hanging limply open. Unfazed, Glen cracked Chris's head into the wall, a rock collapsing his temple and painting the wall red. The final two hikers, Rob and Nick, hesitated, which allowed time for Glen to pull a knife from his camping gear and open Rob's neck. The blood sprayed onto Nick's face, blinding him and causing him to stagger back and slide down the wall. Rob collapsed to the ground, his wet gasping echoing around the cave. Nick held his hands up, pleading, begging for his life, but his cries fell on deaf ears, and the knife was slammed down into the top of his head.

Blood trickled down Nick's brow and dripped from his nose as he realised what had happened. His eyes rolled back, weak groaning slipping from his limp jaw, and he slumped forward, leaving Glen as the only living thing in the cave. Looking at the carnage, Glen began to drag the corpses of his friends to the shrine. He replaced each skull with the corpses until the husk was nearly surrounded by them. There was only one skull left to replace. Lying down, Glen positioned himself in front of the husk and slit his throat. As he convulsed, the blood from him and his friends seeped towards the husk and pooled around it. The cave sat in silence and darkness, warmed by the opened bodies.

The snap of string was the only thing to be heard.

SLEEP: A LITTLE SLICE OF DEATH

Week 1
The first time the Shadow appeared, I had woken up paralysed, stuck to my bedding. Its glowing eyes stared at me, unblinking, unmoving, drilling into me. I began to sweat, trying to move, willing my arm to move, to turn on the light, but it was no use. I was stuck, staring at it. It was staring at me. After maybe hours, the eyes finally sunk back into the darkness.

I shot up, freed from my paralysis, and collapsed off my bed, my breath coming in uneven waves. Flicking on the light, I stared wide-eyed at the empty corner of my room, which had no sign of anyone having been there. The eyes returned every night, staying for longer every time.

Week 2
It started moving. The eyes were getting closer.

First, the eyes returned as usual: me paralysed, sweat dripping down my face, sticking my shirt to my chest. Then, they moved higher. I didn't believe it, unsure that my mind wasn't playing tricks on me. I squeezed my eyes shut as tightly as I could, then blinked quickly, to make sure my sight was clear. It was. And the eyes *had* drifted higher. They slowed to a stop, staring down at me from a higher point on the wall. Then disappeared. Then the next night, they appeared at the height they had reached the previous night. This time, they moved left, creeping closer to me, a creaking moan quietly rising from darkness. Over the week, they got closer and closer to me. Sunday night, they were above me. I craned my eyes up, just being able to see their dull glow. The moan started to increase in volume, getting louder. Louder. Unbearable. I screamed. It disappeared.

Week 3
It has been absorbing darkness.

The eyes had returned to their old position opposite me. I think they had been staying longer than they usually do. I broke eye contact and stared at the abyss of the ceiling. That's when I noticed the darkness slowly retreating from the corners of my room, starting to collect in the centre of the ceiling. Night 2, the darkness seeped towards the eyes and dissolved into the darkness of that wall. A broken chuckle echoed from the eyes.

The walls were next. Deep, heaving breaths forced their way out of the darkness as the Shadow pulled the darkness from the walls. The paint became visible but seemed muted, somehow colourless. As I squinted at the eyes, it looked like they had moved forward, out of the wall. Towards me. My breath quickened, and I slammed my eyes shut. Something was breathing on my face. It was close.

Week 4
I knew it was there before I opened my eyes.

My muscles had cramped, turned to stone. I was paralysed again. Flicking my eyes open, I slowly looked into the darkness, being greeted again by the eyes. The Shadow had already drawn in the darkness from my room, the eyes floating in a black mass opposite me. Two arms creaked from the darkness and planted their hands on the walls either side. The arms were longer and fragile, moving jaggedly, dripping darkness onto the carpet. The arms pushed against the walls, pulling the Shadow out of the darkness. Its head was long, the scalp trailing darkness like it was dissolving. The mouth hung open, a gaping hole of nothingness. The head rotated around, cracking, sounding like splintering wood, until the eyes settled on me again.

The arms bent backwards, gripping onto the ceiling, raising the Shadow up. It dragged itself across my ceiling, revealing a skeletal torso and ribs coated with a black, skin-like material. This glistened like it was damp, and its legs were similar to its arms, but the knees were bending the wrong way. The Shadow hung over me, its breathing ragged, liquid dripping onto my face.

Without warning, it dropped onto me, its face stopping inches from mine. Its knees pressed into my chest, preventing me from breathing easily. It leant forward and placed its hands on my head, one under my chin, one on my scalp. Its eyes stared at me, empty, without emotion, inching closer, closer. I tried to scream, but I didn't have enough air in my lungs to make a noise. Mocking me, the Shadow's fractured scream rose again from its mouth, causing my ears to ring. Before I could close my mouth, its hand that had been resting on my chin moved up, and it curled its fingers into my mouth, holding it open and then dislocating my jaw. My eyes rolled, I moaned, and its fingers caressed my face. It raised its arm and plunged it into my mouth. I gagged as it continued to force its arm down my throat. Its second arm was added, then its head. It was climbing into me, its chest in making my throat bulge. I could taste blood. It was going to use me. I could feel its nails cutting me, and it was dragging its legs into me. Its feet disappeared down my throat, and my jaw snapped shut.

I awoke the next morning feeling fine. I've stopped sleeping. I could hear it in my head, see it in the shadows. I couldn't keep this up. It wanted me to do things for it. Darkness, it was creeping into my vision. It was coming. All I could see was darkness.

ENLIGHTENMENT

I've been having dreams of a place, a figure calling out to me.

I have been chosen, I was special, it needed me. I *had to* find it. The Truth Teller. It has been drawing me to it, irresistible, powerful. I began my pilgrimage and, every night, it came to me: its voice emanating out of nothing, pleading me to find it. I was the only one to help – it had to be me. As I travelled, it gave me instructions, telling me I was getting closer, urging me on to complete the journey.

You are here.

I found it in a ghost town. Abandoned and dilapidated, rotting from the inside out. Windows were broken and smeared with dirt, roofs were collapsed, and walls were buckling under the weight of time. I found the Truth Teller in a church, after following a well-worn path, which stood out due to its lack of dust. Walking through the open doors, I moved towards the cracked altar, where I found it huddled. The roof had been pierced, and the pews lay sprawled across the ground. The crosses had been scattered and left to collect dust, and the stained-glass windows had been bled of their colour.

The Truth Teller that had been calling to me was shrivelled and malnourished, shaking where it lay. It seemed like a living skeleton, grey and covered in black boils. Its movements caused sharp snapping noises from its joints, and as it craned its neck up to me, I saw that its face was only a thin sheet of skin over its skull. Its hands reached out to me, and I stooped down to grab them. Its long, curved nails dug into my hand as its fingers latched onto me. Before I could react, tendrils tore out from the back of the figure and plunged into my mouth, nose, and ears, and coated my eyes.

He had filled me with ~~lies~~ truth. The darkness he had put me in was heavenly. Was this enlightenment? I saw so much, was told so much. I felt weightless, detached from the world and pressures of life in that moment. The power was so great that it burnt. It sliced through my brain and shot down my limbs, like it was pulling me apart. Then, the pain attacked every nerve. I was convulsing with his power, I felt invincible in his embrace. My skin was splitting, bursting with his gift, my bones buckled and splintered, and I was blessed by my own blood. I was helping him. I was part of something bigger, he was making me –

»»»»»»»»

The figure giggled at my distorted and shrivelled corpse in front of him. It poked and played with my limp body, lifting and dropping my arms, smacking around my head, revelling gleefully in its own strength. It scooped up my blood and smeared it across its body, bathing in another success. Then, leaving my deflated corpse alone, it began to call out to another: another stupid enough to answer the call, another that would die.

Come to me. I need you. You have been chosen. Find me.

WHY ARE MY TEARS BLACK?

Snuffing out the candles, Raph asked, "Do you think it worked?"

"It should've, but I told you that you could buy blood; the pig fucking stinks! Pass me the book."

Turning the book over in his hands, Mike fingered through the blood-stained pages, looking again at the rites and diagrams that had been inscribed. "You know the guy who wrote this died, right? I heard that his hand was a real mess by the end of it. A real alcoholic apparently."

"Uh-huh, great to know. Do you feel anything?"

"No, not really, just an ache mostly."

Sighing in disappointment, Mike sat down, flexing his left hand like it was cramping. Looking down at it, he watched the muscles twitch and move, straining against the skin. He stretched his neck, letting out an audible crack.

"I think I got some of the blood in my eye. I can feel something welling up."

Kill him

Rubbing his eye, he found a black smudge left on his palm. Not mentioning it to Raph, he got up and made his way to the bathroom. Standing in front of the mirror, with his left hand, he pushed his eyelids apart, exposing as much of his eye as possible. A thin black line was visible in the corner of his eye. With his right hand, he scratched gently at it, separating it from his eye. Grabbing it, he began to pull, dragging it out from his eye. It appeared to be a hair, but it kept on going, forcing him to use his left hand to continue to draw it out. Finally, the end snapped out and left him leaning over the sink, gasping and rubbing his eye with his palm.

Returning to the living room, he sat back down and watched Raph continue to wipe up the pig's blood. Sneezing into his hand and catching Raph's attention, he said,

"I feel like I've got a cold."

Uncurling his fingers, he saw that it was covered in a viscous, tar-like, black liquid.

>   Kill him

"Hey, look at this."

Raph peered at his hand, becoming excited. "Shit, it must have worked then!"

"If it has, I don't feel as good as I thought I would."

He tried to clear his throat, but this led to a coughing fit, spluttering up more black liquid. It coated his lips and dripped down his chin. Wiping it off with his sleeve, a sticky, black smudge was left across the bottom of his face.

>   Kill him

Looking at Raph, he was becoming less confident. The black liquid began to stream from his nose, causing him to stand up in surprise. He cupped his hands around his nose, trying to stop the stream of black sludge. More black liquid began bubbling from his ears and pouring from his eyes. He began to splutter and tried to wipe away the liquid, but it wouldn't stop, blinding him and making it hard for him to breathe.

>   Kill him

"What have you done to me?!"

He began to panic, choking on the liquid as his eyes became coated with the sludge. Stumbling around with his hands held out in front of him, he tried to locate Raph.

"Help me!" he tried to say, but it was muffled and distorted by the liquid. He began to scream, dropping to his knees, searching the floor blindly.

Kill him

Kill him

KILL HIM

His fingers found the handle of the knife that they used to kill the pig. Wrapping his fingers around the handle, he began to flail the knife around, swinging wildly for Raph. Raph tried to jump and dodge away, but was pressed against the wall, and the wild swings of the knife opened his neck, spraying blood across the room. The viscous liquid finally filled up the man's throat, and he too collapsed to the ground, his chest convulsing, black liquid trickling from his mouth. As he lay there, a puddle of blood and black liquid began to form, connecting the two men together in the fruit of their mistakes.

THE CAVE

The two divers reached the entrance to the cave, swimming up and climbing onto the cold stone. Flipping on their torches, they began to explore. They noticed the stone was covered in a layer of slime, making it hard to grip onto anything. The pillars, which were dotted around the cave, ranged in size, some thick and sturdy looking, some thin and fragile. One of the divers became distracted by their surroundings and slipped, cutting his hand on a rock. They both turned their attention to his wound, which had begun to ooze blood. With the rest of the cave in darkness, they failed to notice the pillars detaching from the ceiling. They were finally alerted to this when the largest one landed on the cave floor with an echoing thud.

Turning around, the divers were met with the sight of giant worm-like creatures. Eyes were dotted around their bodies, and these began to flick open, shaking off the hard shell that had built up over time. Finger-like appendages sprung out of their sides, their means of movement. The creatures' fronts opened, revealing long, sharp teeth soaked with slime. A long, hard tongue emerged, looking like it had an exoskeleton-like coverage, ending in a sharp tip. Screaming, the divers ran deeper into the cave, the creatures surging towards them. The tongues teased them, grazing their backs as they searched desperately for a method of escape.

Finally, the divers found a small opening and squeezed through it, breathing a sigh of relief as the creatures slammed into the wall. A small one had slid through, though, and once more sent the divers scrambling away. Suddenly, a pincer descended from the darkness and, in one clean movement, decapitated it. Swinging their torches up, they watched as another creature dropped slowly to the floor. Its body was bulging, with strips of bone lining it, holding in a fleshy-looking underside reminiscent of an egg sack. Its two pincers were connected to long tentacles, which snaked towards the divers. The creature's head was attached to a long neck. Its face, though, was comprised of multiple eyes, which lined its head in a long, straight line. It had no visible mouth, as the lower half of its head was covered in squirming tongues.

The uninjured diver began to back away, but the other stood frozen in place, transfixed in horror. The creature's two pincers darted towards him and grabbed him under his arms, lifted him up and tore him in half, showering the remaining diver in blood, as guts and loose bones hit the floor. The creature became occupied with the corpse, lifting it up to its head, the tongues sinking into the man's cavities, causing a wet, slurping sound to ring out throughout the cavern. Wiping blood from his eyes, the last diver continued deeper into the cave, frantically trying to send a message for help through his radio, desperate for a way out. All he found, though, was another creature craving the taste of his flesh.

This creature was vastly different to the others. It walked on four legs as it emerged from a crevasse. Its two back legs had three-toed feet, but it had the dexterity of a human hand. Its front legs ended in sharp tips, and its back was covered with flailing tentacles lined with teeth, excreting an odd slime. Its face had two glowing, bug-like eyes, and its mouth resembled the trunk of an elephant. It peered at the man, who had begun to turn away, and pounced, slicing through his leg. As the man fell to the floor, the tentacles descended on him, curling around his limbs and chest. The teeth sunk into his flesh, and the slime began to burn through his skin. Screaming in agony, the man was flipped to face the creature, watching as its mouth split into sections and wrapped around his head, grating his skin and squeezing it to the point he thought his head would explode. Instead, in one clean movement, the creature tore off his head, pulling it into its mouth and cracking through his skull with a wet crunch, like a nut. The diver's body lay mangled and twitching before it was dragged into the darkness, the next meal for the creatures that inhabited the cave.

»»»»»»»

Unbeknownst to the diver, his cry for help had been heard. A rescue attempt had been put into motion, and eleven men from the coastguard had been assembled to go in search of the divers. They were equipped with tools like buzzsaws, clamps and pickaxes, in case the divers were trapped by a section of the cave that had collapsed.

The rescue team plunged under the waves, illuminating the darkness ahead of them, searching for the cave. As they dived deeper, the water became more oppressive, clamping down on them with cold pressure. They sank lower, until they reached the seabed. Continuing forward, they passed under a large overhang, made from jagged, brutal rock. One man looked up and spotted an air pocket. Signalling to the others, the team swam up and pushed their heads out of the water. Looking around them, they took in the sight of the cave, and, recognising their destination, climbed out.

The men unpacked their equipment, handing it around between them. As they attached their head torches and began illuminating their surroundings, the team's leader, Moore, told them to sound off. Doing this attracted the attention of the worm-like creatures that were now roaming the entrance to the cave, still hungry for blood after the divers' escape. Before the rescuers could react, a large creature, about the size of a fully grown man, surged forward and speared the captain through the chest with its tongue. The man looked down in disbelief as blood started to trickle down his wetsuit, causing him to cough up the dark liquid. The creature drew him squirming to its mouth and, upon trying to pull him into it, broke his back and folded him in half before its jaws clamped closed, severing the lower half of his arms and legs. Immediately the smaller creatures lurched forward, spearing and pulling the limbs into their own mouths.

Horror rippled through the rescuers as the creatures acknowledged their intrusion and lunged towards them, scattering them deeper into the cave. As the men ran through the darkness, they scanned for any way to escape. Their headlamps bounced, sending shadows sprawling across the rock, making it near impossible to decipher what was a shadow and what was an opening. The creatures' tongues lashed out, reaching hopefully towards them, but always falling short. One man saw an opening highlighted with blood but, indifferent to this sign of danger, dove towards it, beckoning for the men to follow. Three men did before the worm-like creatures were once again bearing down on them. The final six rescuers had to retreat away from the opening and back into the cave.

They entered a tunnel, though they didn't realise this, and found the next section of the cave completely submerged. Hopeful that this marked an exit, the men jerked their masks back over their faces and, with a final horrified look at the worms, dived into the water.

»»»»»»»

The four rescuers (Martinez, Hill, Phillips, and Campbell) watched with terror as the rest of their team was chased into the darkness, the light from their headlamps slowly disappearing into the cave. They backed away from the opening, scared to attract the attention of the worms, and scanned their new surroundings. As they looked at the jagged rocks, they noticed a trail of blood. Following it with their eyes, they found the two halves of one of the divers lying limp and bloodless on the floor. Their masks muffled their horrified screams and gags as they stumbled back. Distracted by the corpse, they failed to see the crab creature drop down behind them. It reached out and tried to grab Phillips by the leg, but he pulled away, causing his calf to be torn open. Screaming in pain, he fell to the ground, and the three other men spun around to face the creature. Their eyes widened in terror as they processed the form in front of them. As it reached out again, Campbell activated his saw and swiped at the incoming pincer, slicing the tentacle and making the pincer swing limply from the gash. Black blood spurted from the wound to the sound of the creature screaming. It was so high-pitched that the glass of their masks cracked, and rocks were shaken loose from the cave's roof.

Their courage bolstered, the three uninjured men lunged towards the creature, lashing at it wildly, praying for their saws to make contact with its flesh. One swipe caught the bony ribs that lined its body, drawing out another ear-piercing cry. The men registered this and, together, made a move for the creature's egg-sack-like body, causing its eyes to widen and its pincers to speed towards them. The blades snagged the soft skin of its body and tore right through, spilling a translucent slime from its cavity. Stepping back, the men watched in hushed hope as the crab creature began to sway and stumble, and, eventually, came crashing down to the floor.

Panting, they stood around the fallen creature. After checking that the thing was dead, they turned to help tie up their friend's mangled leg. He writhed on the floor as Hill held him down, and Campbell tied a tourniquet around his leg as tightly as he could, hoping to staunch the bleeding. Martinez kept watch, making sure another creature didn't catch them by surprise again. Once they had attended to Phillips' leg, they pulled him up, each slinging one of the injured man's arms over their shoulders, carrying him between them. As they turned around, they noticed that the previously sagging body of the creature was now rippling, and with dread, they watched its offspring flow out of the drained corpse.

Dragging their friend behind them, they ran from the tidal wave of death and followed the divers' path unknowingly further into the cave. Glancing back, they were met with the sight of hundreds of miniature crab creatures scuttling after them, snapping at them with their pincers. The four rescuers entered another looming cavern within the cave, panting, their hearts pounding to the point of failure. Phillips began to slip from their grasp, but the men had no time to stop and find a better grip, and he fell to the floor behind them. The miniature creatures swarmed his injured leg, tearing at the wrappings. Desperately, Campbell and Hill quickly grabbed Phillips by his armpits and continued to drag him away, shaking off the creatures in the process, as Martinez tried to push the creatures back with the whir of his saw. As they started to drag Phillips away again, the miniature creatures surged forward and swarmed over Martinez, tearing through his wetsuit, sinking through his eyes, filling his mouth, and devouring him in seconds. The remaining three men didn't stop to try and help but carried on running through the cave, trying to put as much distance between them and the waves of death that snapped at their heels. Suddenly, though, the creatures stopped their pursuit and stood still, lining the entrance to the cavern. They snapped and clicked at the men, frantic for their flesh, but something held them back.

The three men stared at the waves of creatures, thankful for the respite from danger. Their breathing slowed and stopped raking at their throats as they backed away, still dragging the injured Philips, and they illuminated the surrounding cavern. They were met with the sight of walls and the ceiling coated in holes and tunnels, looking like a honeycomb, and the deep growls of more creatures. Small dots of glowing red grew larger, and talons exposed themselves to the light made by the men. The first creature landed in front of them, followed by a second, then a third. They prowled around the huddled men, inspecting their prey. The creatures swiped at them, unfurling their horrid mouths, taunting the men.

The three rescuers scanned the surrounding holes in the cave, hoping that one would provide escape. Dropping to the floor, the men evaded the pounce of the first creature, leaving it to skid to a halt behind them. This opened a hole in the creatures' ranks and was a chance that the men would not lose. They ran for a hole that was glistening with moisture, hopefully a sign of water that would facilitate their escape. The rescuers refused to look behind them, terrified at how close the creatures might be. The air became thick with moisture, and the rock became harder to grip. The moisture on the walls changed into a mucus-like substance, thick and viscous, and light began to creep into the tunnel, reflecting off the glistening rock, spurring new hope into the defeated men. Bounding towards the light, they entered another vast cavern. Before the men could take in their surroundings, though, the creatures leapt out of the darkness and once more prowled towards them. The men were backed against the edge of a lake which spanned most of the cavern. The water behind them rippled, eliciting a high-pitched whine from the creatures. They began to back off, slinking back into the darkness like spurned children.

The men collapsed onto the stone, finally alone. They stared in amazement at the environment, clicking off their lights as the glow from their surroundings easily lit the cavern. The crystals that jutted out of the walls shone with brilliant purple, semi-translucent, unearthly. Thick vines hung from the cavern roof, dripping with condensation. The men looked down into the deep water that sat in front of them, searching for any sign of an exit. The water itself glowed, almost pulsated with pure blue light. The blue aura leaked from the water, repainting the men's faces blue, as if there were a light source hidden in its depths. Small creatures flitted past their eyes. Scaly tadpole-like beings with two heads darted close to the water's edge; fish with flowing manes tipped with light teased the small lifeforms but were slapped away by what looked like seaweed as thick as a piece of cardboard, which seemed to angle itself towards the creatures, as if watching their antics.

Breaking away from their awe, the men reached for their radios and tried to contact the rest of their team.

"One diver is dead. We located a corpse – and given the monsters that we ran into – I doubt the other one is still alive… We are in a large, brightly lit cavern… Try and find us and then we need to leave. There are more creatures in here! One of them got Martinez. Phillips is injured. We need help! We are not fucking equipped for this."

Placing the radio down, Campbell laid back on the stone, letting his mind wander, waiting for a reply. Looking around him again, he noticed that he was alone. Sitting up, he couldn't see the other two men. The only sign of them having been with him was a trail of blood, which ended by the water. As he stood up, anxiety and fear began to strangle him once more, and a large black shadow started to invade the water. As he stumbled back in alarm, a giant creature burst from the water, silhouetted against the water's glow, and dived down at the rescuer.

»»»»»»»»

Flicking their lights on, the other six men from the rescue team turned in the water, waiting to see if the worms would follow their lead and join them underwater. The silhouettes of the creatures were visible, staring down at them, whipping the water with their tongues. After waiting for a couple of minutes, it became clear that the creatures were not going to leave the water's edge, and were still hellbent on their flesh. Realising this, the divers turned and swam further into the water-filled passage.

They swam uninterrupted through the flooded passage, stopped only by a wall that signalled the end of the path. Looking around, it became clear that now the only way left to go was down. They sank deeper into the bowels of the cave system, food for larger creatures than themselves. As they dropped down into the new section of the cave, bright green vines and plant life began to appear on the rocks that surrounded them. Hitting the new bottom, the divers saw that their path forward was littered with the long, swaying forms of thick seaweed. Looking at each other, they agreed to carry on forward, hopeful of finding the rest of their team.

As they approached the seaweed, a sense of trepidation began to grip them. It seemed to sway towards them, but their distrust of the plants was interrupted by the crackle of their radios.

"Diver ... dead. Located a corpse ... monsters that we ran into ... still alive. Large ... cavern ... need to leave."

The broken sound of their teammate's voice instilled new hope into the men, and unable to respond, they decided to press forward into the forest of yellow-spotted seaweed.

The men slipped between the foliage, trying to avoid touching it. A diver in the middle of their group accidentally kicked one of the strands, which triggered it to wrap around his ankle. He turned around, pulling at the plant, trying to break free. His struggles were noticed by the others, and soon, the group had gathered around, trying to free him. The seaweed began to squeeze tighter, eliciting a sharp cry of pain from the man, who began to thrash and flail as the pain grew and grew and grew until it built to the muffled but clearly audible snap of his ankle. The force moved the diver, and his writhing caused him to hit more of the seaweed. Instantly, the plant coiled around his arms, twisting and crushing, snapping one backwards and tearing the other clean off, clouding the men's vision with diluted blood. Sickened by this sight, a younger rescuer backed into another plant, causing it to embrace his torso. The snapping of ribs like twigs could be heard, and, hoping for a quicker and less painful death, the man removed his mask, and the others were forced to watch their friend drown, unable to help, unable to attack the seaweed without attracting the attention of more foliage. Silently, they continued, leaving the two floating corpses behind them, enveloped by a mist of blood, restarting their acrobatics around the plants.

Reaching the end of the field of death, the remaining divers were greeted by a strange, distant source of light. As they got closer to it, they felt the water increase in temperature, and a deep resonating pulse began to wash over them. The water seemed to pulsate around them, like a heartbeat, as if it were alive. The water glowed a bright blue, picturesque in appearance, in juxtaposition to the colour of death which infested the cave. They passed over what appeared to be the source of the strange light, stopping and staring at what greeted them. A gaping mouth lay on the deepest section of the cave, sucking in and blowing out water rhythmically, like the rise and fall of a chest. The light emanated from its depths, shining into the water, revealing the tentacle-like structures that framed it. A film covered its hollow centre, which was being pushed against by some unknown being; only vague shapes could be seen through its opaqueness. Unsettled by its womb-like appearance, the rescuers moved on, shuddering from the idea of meeting whatever was on the other side of it.

Realising they were able to rise, they slowly drifted up, passing strange fish and micro-lifeforms, and smaller versions of the seaweed they had encountered, a stark reminder of their need to escape. Breaking the surface, they swam to the edge of the lake and pulled themselves out. Looking around at the vines and crystals, the men hoped that this was close to where the others were. Pulling out a radio, one man tried to contact the other group but was only met with static. The static they heard, though, was coupled with the echo of static elsewhere in the cavern. Making their way towards the noise, they found an abandoned radio. Hopeful this meant the rest of them were nearby, they began to scan their environment more closely, praying for a sign the other rescuers had been here. Noticing a flipper partially covered by shrubbery, they made their way over, relief flooding their bodies. Giving it a tug, assuming the man it belonged to was only asleep, the flipper was pulled from the bush, along with a severed leg which hung limply from the ankle. Staggering back, the divers found more remains – masks, fingers, blood, chunks of flesh. The four men began to drown in despair, failing to notice the surface of the lake beginning to ripple.

Out of the water rose a giant creature whose shadow threw the cavern into darkness. It resembled an eel, with slick, dark-purple skin, which was pulled taut over a bulging muscular structure. Its eyes were bottomless pinpricks of blackness, which seemed to steal light from the surroundings. The creature's back was lined with curved and sharp, deep-red, bone-reinforced spines, rippling with hatred for the men. Its mouth curled open, revealing two first rows of thin, wickedly pointed teeth still flecked with blood from its previous meal. As these parted, a second mouth was revealed, but this one was rotated by 90 degrees and parted sideways. The teeth on this one were shorter and thicker, but still razor-sharp. The mouths dripped with saliva and allowed the creature's tongue to unfurl and whip at the air in front of the men. Its screech dislodged stone from the ceiling and caused the men to drop to their knees. They pressed their hands into their ears in a desperate attempt to block out the noise. The creature dived down towards them, snatching one of the men in its jaws, and as the many sets of teeth closed, he was pulverised, like fruit in a blender, and only blood leaked from the thing's mouth, spilling out between its teeth.

In an awe-inducing terror, the last three men ran from the creature, pressing themselves against the wall of the cavern. It swung down again, trying to reach them. It roared and lashed its tongue, furious it couldn't reach the men. They pressed their heads onto the stone, wishing they could merge with it, praying that they would escape. The creature withdrew and then, with all its might, lunged again but stopped short, like a dog on a chain as something was holding it back. As it pulled and strained against the unseen restriction, the cavern seemed to heave and shudder; the water became violent, spilling onto the stone and, finally, rushing up in a geyser. Sand and stone flew with it, like hail, showering the men and making them cower with their arms covering their heads.

Freed from its natural entrapment, the creature stretched and flung its limbs across the cavern, filling the space. It had finally unearthed its many tentacles, each flowering into mouths. Starfish-like limbs grew out of the four corners of each of these, with opposable black talons curving over the mouths in between each starfish-like limb. The mouths of the tentacles themselves were filled with small teeth, like each tentacle was its own creature, separate from the whole. As the creature climbed out of the water, it became clear to the rescuers what it truly was. Although its top half resembled an eel, it was much closer to a giant octopus or squid, with its many tentacles.

As they turned to run, one of the tentacles surged down and latched on to a rescuer's shoulder, the limbs curling around his neck and the talons sinking into his flesh. He screamed as blood trickled down his chest, and the other two rescuers turned and, using rocks, hammered at the limb until it came loose. A gaping hole was left, bone sticking out, and his arm hung down, connected to his body only by flaps of skin. A second tentacle came screaming down and bit down on his side, followed by another on the opposite side, and a fourth came and tore off the man's mangled arm, flinging it into the creature's gaping mouth. The two tentacles attached to his sides quickly pulled away from him, tearing off chunks of his flesh, exposing his organs, and leaving him feebly trying to keep them in his body, but he soon succumbed to his wounds and collapsed into a pile of his own guts.

Turning once more to try and escape it, the next man found a tentacle sinking its talons into his temples and lifting him off the floor. His eyes rolled as the teeth worked their way through his skull, and unintelligible sounds escaped his mouth as he was dropped into the creature's mouth, reduced to a fine mist by its countless teeth. The final man picked up a saw which had been left lying in the water by the other men and turned, determined to cause the creature some pain. As another mouthed tentacle approached him, he swung at it, slicing one of its limbs clean off. Thick blood oozed from the wound, and the creature screeched in response. A barrage of tentacles followed and picked the man up. He continued to carve at the limbs madly, having accepted his death. Furious with the pain the man was causing, the creature slammed the rescuer into the roof of the cavern with as much force as it could. A rock caved in the man's head, and small crystals lodged into his chest. Although he died immediately, the creature dragged the man across the uneven roof, shredding layers off the corpse until it fell apart in its grip.

The force of the impact had caused water to start leaking into the cavern from outside. The creature spotted it and continued to probe the cavern's weakness. It slammed into and threw rocks at the hole, turning the leak into a stream, then into a shower, then into a tidal wave as the sea flooded into the cavern. As the water level rose, so did the creature. It grew closer and closer to the hole until it shot its limbs through it and pulled itself up to it, slamming its head into the rock. It pushed and strained against it until the hole gave in and burst, flinging the creature into the sea. The cavern began to collapse, opening itself to the outside world. As the giant creature floated and watched this happen, it began to turn and look to the surface. Gnashing its teeth, it drove upwards, looking for the surface, looking for land, looking for food.

MASKS OF STOLEN SKIN

The following document is the transcript of the final session between Dr. Miles Bennell and Patient #2911 before the patient's believed escape.

Start of recording

Doctor: Are you aware that our session is being recorded?

Patient: Yes.

Doctor: And do you consent to the recording?

Patient: Yes.

Doctor: Great, thank you. Ok, so how are we feeling today?

Patient: I'm looking forward to being transferred to a more relaxed place and losing this straitjacket.

Doctor: Quite understandable, but it was for your own safety. By the time you were delivered to us, you were fully engulfed in your paranoid delusions.

On this subject, before you can be transferred, we need to make sure you understand that your beliefs were, in fact, purely delusions. So, if you could, in as much detail as possible, recount them to me?

Patient: Sure, from the beginning?

Doctor: From the beginning.

(Patient pauses and sighs)

Patient: Ok, well, it started after I was attacked in an alley. A man had jumped me and was trying to mug me, so I tried to poke his eyes, but instead of him drawing back, I thought that I had pulled off his face, like a mask. In my panicked state, I demonised him, and in my mind, he had been a creature in disguise.

Doctor: And what did this creature look like?

Patient: His eyes had no eyelids, and the veins in his eyes writhed like worms. He had a wide smile, with layers of overlapping teeth. Instead of a nose, there was only a hole, from which a long, forked tongue emerged. His true skin was peeling and resembled the skin of a burn victim.

Doctor: And that is…?

Patient: Not real. My mind was filling in the gaps in my memory from the attack.

Doctor: Good, please continue.

Patient: After the attack, I began to become paranoid. I was convinced there was a race of creatures that were using people's skin to blend in.

Doctor: Quite rightly.

Patient: I'm sorry?

Doctor: Quite rightly you believed it. You were traumatised, after all.

Patient: Right. Well, as time went on, I began to feel watched, like I was under surveillance. I reached the conclusion that the creatures were watching me, waiting to attack me again because I knew of their existence.

Doctor: And what did you do?

Patient: I shut myself in, stopped leaving my home and cut off all communication with my family, which caused them concern.

Doctor: Did your self-imposed isolation help relieve these feelings?

Patient: No, I felt like I was being surrounded, or cornered.

Doctor: This all reached its limits when your family arrived, yes?

Patient: I had destroyed the phones, so I had no idea that they were coming.

Doctor: Ok, and your family's arrival is what triggered your violent breakdown?

Patient: It was. They arrived in a group, three of them, my sister, my aunt, and my mother, I think. I initially trusted them, and recounted my beliefs to them, after which they called me 'crazy'. I snapped and accused them of being creatures, and lunged at my mother, sinking my nails into her cheeks and tearing off strips of her skin in an attempt to prove their lack of humanity. My aunt tried to pull me away, but I spun and, in another attempt to unmask them, scratched through my sister's eyes. The final one had blocked the door, but I rushed them, grabbed their lower lip, and pulled it off, taking off the skin on their chin as well.

Doctor: Why did you aim for her lip?

Patient: The creatures don't have lips, so I thought it would be the quickest way to prove my aunt wasn't human. She was also blocking the door, so I had no doubt that she was not who I thought she was.

(Patient breathes heavily)

Doctor: Ok, so what happened after you left the house?

Patient: One of my relatives had called the police when I was struggling with the last relative, so they arrived as I was leaving the house. A couple of police officers tried to restrain me, but I managed to injure them in the same manner as my relatives.

Doctor: Do you remember the paramedic you killed?

Patient: It was the first one to come out of the ambulance. I broke free from the officers, and as he was about to inject a sedative, I grabbed the skin behind both sides of his jaw and ripped it off, skinning the lower half of his face. I was told he went into shock and suffocated on his own tongue.

Doctor: Correct. And then you were sedated and brought here, where I started your treatment.

(Pause. Doctor clears his throat)

Doctor: So, what do you think these creatures are doing now?

Patient: Nothing, they do not exist.

Doctor: Excellent. You have made great progress.

Patient: When will I be transferred then?

Doctor: Tomorrow, I believe. There is just one last thing that I need to do first.

(Something is dropped to the floor. Patient begins to hyperventilate)

Patient: They *are* real! You, you tricked me! Get away from me, GET AWAY! I WILL KILL YOU, STAY AWAY!

Doctor: Nurse! He is relapsing into his delusion. I was wrong, he needs more treatment. He'll need another round of Electroshock Therapy, at a higher voltage this time. Don't worry, I'll help you, I won't let your delusions control you. I will save you.

End of recording

BEFORE...

I lifted my face to the sky, showing Him my work, my dedication. I pinned it to the wall, a symbol of the sin I had defeated, along with the bin full of my skin. Euphoria coursed through my form. I glistened with Holy Glory.
  He is coming.
  I am here.
  The skinned man stared at his form in exultation, revelling in his transformation. He cried and thanked Him, and he was filled with the feeling of triumph; he had reached his true form. Behind him, out of the darkness, unnoticed, strode The Creator, his hands clasped behind his back. The Creator stood, towering over the man, silent and watching curiously the jubilation of the skinless man. The Creator was humanoid in form and had bandages covering his head, with slight indents and bumps hinting at a human-like face underneath. Around his neck hung a pendant in the form of a headless woman. His clothing was formed of intricate, gold metalwork, snaking around his form like he was wearing armour. Over this, a dark purple robe was fastened around his neck, pinned together with the head of a woman. The robe clung tightly to his shoulders, creating the impression that his shoulders were pointed. His hands were exposed and were the clearest sign of The Creator's inhuman origin. His skin looked like it was rotting, welts dotted on the tops of his hands. The veins in them also writhed under his skin, like snakes, and his nails were pointed and crusted with dirt and blood.
  Finally spotting the figure, the skinless man spun to face him,

furious at his intrusion. "Who the fuck are you?" the man spat, feeling violated by the unexpected visitor.

"Do you not recognise your God, the one that you 'transformed' for?"

The man's jaw hung slack, and with wide eyes, he dropped to his knees, bowing his head. "I–I'm sorry, master. I wasn't expecting you so soon. I–I hope you are pleased. I did this for you. I am your servant; I live thanks to your gift."

"What you have done is impressive."

"Thank y–"

"Impressive, but insolent. How dare you defile my name with your actions! What you have done disgusts me. Your false act of faith is like poison. You are truly pathetic, you think that–"

The man sank lower, The Creator's words landing like knives in his heart. "But this is your will. Your gift allowed me to do this for you, you chose me."

"Your hubris is unmatched."

Saying this, The Creator leant down and wrapped his hands around the man's mouth and effortlessly dislocated his jaw. Surprise overtook the man, and he lurched back, holding his hanging jaw. His tongue flapped as he tried to speak, but only distorted moans escaped. The Creator strode towards him, causing him to back away and press himself against the wall. The Creator bent down until his face was level with the man's and continued his speech.

"You are tainted, dirty flesh. You do not have the true strength that a transformation requires. You do not have a gift. You have merely been marked as unworthy. You are meant for nothing, but instead, your self-absorbed mind has allowed you to believe that you can ascend higher than you are deserving of. You disgust me. You only possess false strength, a shadow of the potential that other humans have. You cannot begin to understand what it means to sacrifice, to give in to your pain. It is pathetic. Your crude instruments insult mine; your discarded skin is like faeces. You sacrificed nothing. It cost you nothing to strip off your skin: you had no agony, no pain, not even discomfort. You have cheated. You have taken it upon yourself to insult a god, not worship one. There are those who try and use their abilities to please me: surgeons who are trying to create new beings with wasted flesh, or those using medicines to empower new generations, but you squander this. But you have the chance to find redemption. You can still prove that you are worthy to be my lowest creation, my lowest soldier. I can give you pain. I can let you feel what you have done, but you cannot fail this again. You will see more than you deserve and get more than you deserve."

The man nodded feverishly, tears streaming down his face. Reaching out, The Creator pushed his jaw back into its sockets and waited for the man's response.

"Please, let me prove myself to you! I thought I was doing your will; I would not dream of disgracing you. I will pass your tests; I want to serve!"

"We shall see."

Without any further words, The Creator granted the skinless man the ability to experience his pain. Immediately, the man seized, jolting and jerking against the wall. The Creator stepped away from him, watching with amusement as the man slipped to the floor. Animalistic, distorted, and piercing shrieks began to flow out of the man. Everything that touched his raw muscles sent shards of agony scraping along his body. The man climbed to his feet, trying to show strength, but as he stood there, every second his stripped feet touched the floor, another eternity of pain was sent shooting through his body. He tried to hold himself, but as his bare arms touched his bleeding chest, another army of pain trampled across his nerves. He jerked his arms apart, but the muscles had stuck to each other, so in the process, he had to tear his arms apart, something which proved a nearly impossible task. He fell back to the floor, but his state made the cold hardwood feel like molten glass shards were carving into his back. As he rolled around on the floor, he couldn't escape the pain. Every micro-movement only increased it, every blink felt like his eyes were melting, every scream felt like his throat would pull itself apart. The pain embraced him in its agonising embrace. His response to The Creator's disgust was to vomit; it slid onto the floor, causing The Creator to step back further. Finally, in a puddle of his vomit, the man passed out, beaten into submission by his pain.

Sighing in expected disappointment, The Creator stepped towards the man's unconscious form, avoiding the vomit, and reached out, pressing his finger to the man's forehead. With a gasp, the man awoke, jolting upright and coughing out the last of his sick, clearing his throat. He did not speak for a few moments. Instead, he sat panting, staring intensely at the floor, refusing to meet The Creator's burning gaze.

"I'm sor–"

> "You pitiful creature. You have clearly failed me but simply cannot accept it. You are truly pathetic, unworthy of my help or guidance. What more proof do you need of your failure?"

"I'm sorry, I can handle it, I promise. I wasn't prepared for what your test entailed. I can handle it. I can–"

As he trailed off, The Creator tilted the man's head up to look at his overbearing form.

> "You cannot, and you do not learn.
> You are just embarrassing yourself."

With that, The Creator reached into the man's mouth and tore out his tongue. It hung limply from his hand, scraps of muscle swinging from the end of it, dripping blood onto the floor. The man's gurgling scream burst out of his blood-filled mouth, and he watched in horror as it began to spill out of his mouth and pool in his lap.

"Your tongue was doing you no good. You didn't even know how to use it. Luxuriate in the peace this has brought. The world is no longer troubled by your useless ramblings."

The Creator stood up, dropping the torn tongue and wiped his hand on his robe. He turned to leave, but on second thought, he turned back and once more addressed the defeated man.

"I will show you my true disciples. Those who have passed my tests, true victors. This will be the only way the gravity of your actions will weigh on your shoulders. This will finally destroy your hubris. You will see your failure."

Gesturing for the man to follow him, The Creator walked back into the darkness. The man scrambled to his feet, wiping the blood from his mouth and spitting out as much as he could. Walking through the darkness, The Creator silently led the way, ignoring the man's increasing discomfort. The man began to feel hot, the damp layer over his muscles started to steam, and as they exited the darkness, he was no longer glistening and was now dry, every movement causing slight discomfort.

"Even you are not able to evade pain here. Here, you will never rest in comfort again."

Looking over his shoulder at the way they had come, the man saw nothing but the orange-tinged expanse of The Creator's laboratory. It was filled with cages, some filled with horrific, mutilated, and bloody creatures rattling their bars, and tubes filled with liquid, with small creations floating in them, some with plant life spotted with yellow. Dissection tables were covered with the corpses of dissected and gutted things. Some looked human, others were barely recognisable as animals. The skinned man approached one creature, which was splayed open on one of The Creator's tables. Its face was twisted, with its jaw hanging down at an unnatural angle. Its limbs looked like they had been twisted backwards, broken string dangled from its skin, and its torso was folded open, its organs lying next to it, still fully connected, pinned to the work surface. As the man leant in, the creature shuddered back to life, its head turning to him, releasing maniacal laughter, its tongue licking wildly at him. Disturbed, the man backed away, returning to follow The Creator.

> "Now that you are done meddling with my children, I will show you what you could have been if you were not so weak. You will see the successes, people worthy of my cause. You will see a man fresh out of his tests. A man that sees more than you have ever seen."

Leaving The Creator's laboratory, the two entered a humid environment, tinged orange by the sulphur-infused clouds. The clouds looked like bursts of flame, burning the discoloured sky. On the rocky embankments surrounding the path that the two were walking down, elongated and ungodly creatures darted past them, stopping at a safe distance on all fours, their black manes quivering, watching their progression eagerly. Screams and cries were heard in the distance, a ghastly choir of pain which The Creator tilted his head back to enjoy. The skinless man, however, jumped at the howls and screams, unease building as he looked over his shoulder at the creatures which followed them. The Creator diverted them off the path, walking up and into a cave. Rocks hung menacingly from the ceiling, poised to fall and impale the skinless man. With every step he took, rocks stabbed into his exposed foot, causing him to leave bloody footprints in the dust behind him. As they descended into the darkness, The Creator removed his hands from behind his back, held them, palm up, on either side of him and unfurled his fingers. From the centre of his palms emanated two fires, lighting the way before them, the skinless man quickening his steps to stay close to The Creator's light. They reached the end of the tunnel, a solid wall of rock. On The Creator's approach, though, the rocks parted, and from the light of his hands, the skinless man saw a long, dark corridor.

As they stepped into the corridor, the skinless man winced at the increase in temperature. He was quickly distracted, though, by the unhinged laughter that was echoing out of the darkness. The laughter was contorted with a cry of pain. The skinless man squinted into the darkness, trying to find the source of the noise, but was interrupted by The Creator.

> "Come to me, my child. You have seen the glory I bring. You have seen what I have seen. You have done so well. Your time has come to join me."

Addressing the skinless man now, The Creator explained what was approaching.

> "He is worthy. He has been purified by his pain. A purification that few can understand. A purification that you cheated."

The thing that The Creator had called to finally reached his light, scrabbling forward through the darkness. The skinless man was disgusted to see another man that was horribly mutilated. His eyes were spread down his cheeks, and as his head tilted to the warmth of The Creator's light, the man could see chunks of his eyes that lay uselessly in their sockets. His chest and body were covered in burst blisters and scored by the torn trenches of missing flesh. The man grinned maniacally up at The Creator, seemingly happy to see him. The skinned man moaned in protest, turning to The Creator.

> "No, you are insane, rotting with delusion.
> He sees the truth; he sees my vision!"

As he said this, The Creator reached down and took the disfigured man by the hand and helped him to his feet. He began to leave the corridor, leading the disfigured man by his side, but as he reached the exit, he turned and stopped the skinless man from following.

> "This is where you will learn. We shall see how long it takes for you to understand. An eternity of pain is all you will ever know."

As he said this, the skinless man fell to the floor, screaming and seizing in pain. As the man touched the walls, his flesh sizzled and burned, and left him convulsing on the floor of the corridor.

> "You are nothing. You wanted things you had no right to want. This is more than what you deserve. This is all you shall have."

The Creator turned and left, leading the disfigured man out of the corridor and into the cave. As they left, the entrance closed, leaving the skinless man screaming and shrieking in agony in solitary, endless darkness.

»»»»»»»

Guiding the disfigured man by the hand, The Creator led him carefully out of the cave. He didn't turn to watch the convulsing, skinless man reaching out for him as the rocks closed off the entrance to the corridor once more, and once it had been closed, the screaming was cut off abruptly, letting The Creator and the disfigured man leave in peace. The disfigured man tripped and stumbled on the uneven surface of the cave, with The Creator trying to hold him up as they made their way towards the path and towards his laboratory.

As they progressed down, the quadrupedal creatures jumped and screamed around them, following their progress. They never leapt in front of The Creator and always made sure to stay behind him, revelling in his wake. The disfigured man craned his face towards the burning sky, smiling uncontrollably at the heat it gave off. He clung tightly to The Creator's outstretched arm, guiding him forward.

They entered The Creator's laboratory, leaving the creatures behind as they lined the outside of the building. He sat the disfigured man down on a table and stood in front of him, taking in the man's warped figure.

"You are a success, my child. You have endured so much and done so well. You let my voice guide you to the end of the pain, and let my vision embrace you. I am regretful to tell you that more is to come, though. More pain, more hardship. It is necessary for my world to become physical, tangible. I must prepare you for your final challenge. Once I have done this, I will leave and set more cogs into motion, let the clock get closer to midnight. My time, your time, is fast approaching. Do not stray from my path."

During this, the disfigured man sat and lolled his head and smiled at The Creator. Seemingly satisfied with his answer, The Creator reached forward and placed his hands on either side of the man's face. He then plunged his thumbs into the man's eye sockets and dug out the remainder of the man's eyes, pushing the chunks onto the floor. Once he was satisfied with this, he pushed his thumbs deeper, straining slightly against the bone at the back of the man's sockets until, with a crack, he broke through, and his thumbs sank deeper into the man's head, stopping short of piercing his brain. Content with this, he placed one hand on the back of the man's head, placed his other on the man's chest, and guided him to lay down on the table. To prevent the man from moving, he pinned him down by striking nails through his hands and feet, spreading him across it like a taxidermied butterfly.

The Creator examined the uneven, intertwining maze of deep

trenches of missing flesh that adorned the disfigured man's torso. He used his gleaming tools to probe the burst blisters, working out how deep these wells of pus had penetrated the man. He ran his finger through the length of the trenches, mapping out in his mind the full maze of his wounds. Once he was satisfied with his examination, he took out his beautifully decorated and shining knife and began to refine the maze of missing flesh on the man's chest. He started by slicing away any ragged edges that the man's fingers had left, discarding slices of his flesh like it was rotten bacon. Now the wounds had straight, sharp edges, The Creator moved on to crafting one singular pathway through the trenches. He carved out chunks of flesh, connecting pathways and creating a snaking path across the man's chest.

In places, The Creator deepened the wounds, advancing further and, in other places, exposing parts of the man's organs. Once The Creator had perfected his winding route through the man's torso, he returned his attention to the various burst blisters which littered the small amount of untouched skin that remained on the man. Blisters that he felt were too shallow he left alone. He was going to return to them when he was completing his finishing touches, but for the few that were deep, he widened the entrance to them and deepened the holes, curving them around so that they connected and opened to the newly crafted pathway. Stepping back, The Creator carefully examined his work, checking inch by inch that it was accurate and precise. The time for mistakes had long passed.

Placing blocks to section off his pathway, he isolated the unneeded trenches that the man had made. In these, he placed blocks of metal, and igniting the flames in his hands, he melted the blocks, eliciting a warped scream from the man. Once the metal had melted and filled up the useless holes, he placed winding and contorted black metal in the liquid, and once it had cooled and hardened, the man was left branded by the mark of The Creator, black snake-like figures now adorning his chest. The man lay panting, recovering from the ordeal as The Creator placed more metal over the man's chest, leaving his pathway uncovered, and with long, curved nails, fastened the metal to the man's flesh. When the work was finally finished and he was satisfied, The Creator stepped back and spoke once more to the disfigured man, now perfected.

> "You are meant for more, so much more. I have now prepared you to fulfil this, to serve me and help realise my vision of perfection. You are the perfect vessel, the perfect ingredient. I must retrieve what will make you complete, what is meant to be yours to help me command. The pieces are nearly in place. Soon, so soon, our time will come. I must leave you now, but relish in the light, relish in your form. You are not alone, I have surrounded you with my other creations, your brothers. You must gather your strength for the final part of your challenge. Soon, you will feel true light, true freedom. Once I return, you will be able to make me proud. The final tracks must be laid."

With that, The Creator left his creation, who was smiling and laughing maniacally at The Creator's words, eager and gleeful at The Creator's promise. Striding away from the disfigured man, The Creator entered the darkness, entering its embrace, ready to guide his most uncontrollable creations to their true purpose, what he had made them for.

»»»»»»»

The insectoids filled the town, spilling into every street, every home, every head. Soon, the town could not hold them. Soon nothing would.

The Creator arrived next to where he had left his insectoid queen, in a crater in the forest. Looking around, he spotted the corpse of a man and crouched down next to it, examining the body. He noticed that the man's hands were cut open; many small but deep cuts decorated his hands and forearms. Moving up to the head, he saw that the man's lips had been sliced to ribbons. They dangled in front of his teeth, barely covering them. Looking into the mouth, a dissected tongue greeted him, with more lacerations coating the back of the man's throat. Switching his attention to the most obvious damage, The Creator began to probe the man's blown-out chest. Moving any hanging pieces from the hole, he was able to see the internal damage that his insectoid had caused. The man's stomach had been completely torn open, like a broken bag, and its contents were left to seep across his organs. His bottom ribs had been broken, and others showed signs of damage; chunks of them were missing. Although, at first glance, the man's chest looked like it had been viciously torn open, The Creator saw that all the cuts were clean and sharp. Content with what his creation had done, he did one final examination of the area. A puddle of blood caught his attention; it lay glittering in the moonlight. This pleased him. It was a sign that the insectoid had been able to procreate and its offspring had survived the incubation within the man. Spurred on by this sign, The Creator began the walk into the town that he had used as a breeding ground for his insectoids.

Walking through the forest, The Creator was met with pure silence. No animals could be heard rustling the bushes, no birds could be seen in the sky. The Creator was alone. The lights of the town were still on, a beacon for his progress, leaking between the trees, beckoning him forward. Excitement was filling him, increasing with every step The Creator took towards the town and his creations. Finally breaking out from the trees, The Creator stood on the edge of a silent town. He continued into the centre and paused, admiring the scene. The cobbled paving was coated in a thin layer of blood, shining red under the streetlights. Strewn across the centre, though, were chunks of flesh, torn eagerly from the inhabitants. The odd foot, hand, fingers, and heads also littered the floor, frozen in abject terror at their premature deaths. Completing the picture of chaos were the vehicles. Cars had their windows smashed in, dusting the floor with shards of glass. Windshields were caved in, and small holes adorned them, evidence of the insectoids' rampage. Cars had also crashed into buildings, caving in walls and destroying windows of shop fronts.

A few streetlights had also been damaged; some cars had wrapped themselves around them, tilting them precariously towards the ground.

This all pleased The Creator. He was overjoyed with the success of his creations; they had propagated and evolved quickly and showed their strength, adaptability, and hunger, a tool which would prove invaluable to The Creator's crusade. The Creator's thoughts were stopped short, though, by the sharp whispering of a man. Looking around, he spotted a dirty and dishevelled man crouching in a house, beckoning for The Creator to come to him. Curiously, The Creator approached and stood in front of the hiding man. The Creator was hidden by darkness, leading the man to believe he had found another survivor. Urgently and in a hushed tone, the man addressed The Creator.

"Are you crazy? You can't just stand in the open, they will see you, and once they do, you are fucked. They have killed everyone, these, these horrific things. They just appeared and tore through everything. There was nothing we could do. We are stuck. I was with a few others, they made a break for it, but I watched with my own eyes as they were torn apart by those abominations. You need to hide!"

"Abominations?"

The Creator inquired as he leant into the light, allowing the man to see his form. Terrified, the man backed away. The Creator began to stride towards him, crushing rubble of broken walls under his feet, throwing plumes of dust into the air.

"I would hope that it is not safe, otherwise I have truly failed with these creations. All you should talk about is a success, no horrific things, no abominations, just success. From just one singular insectoid, your town has been slaughtered and destroyed. Unfortunately, I was unable to stay and watch the fun. Your survival is surprising, but it gives me an unexpected opportunity. You can show me how my creations have flourished."

The Creator grabbed the man by the neck, effortlessly lifted him off his feet, and carried him into the centre of the town. The man struggled and kicked and punched The Creator. None of these proved to be effective, though, and only served to make The Creator tighten his grip on the man, slowly choking the life out of him with every strained gasp that the man let out. Now positioned in the centre, The Creator loosened his grip on the man's neck, holding him by the shoulder. Wrapping his other hand around the man's arm, he brutally snapped it, letting the sound resonate around the desolate square. The bone had torn through the man's skin and jabbed into the open air, dripping with blood. The man screamed, puncturing the silence, and The Creator tossed him down, causing him to roll as he hit the ground. The man sat with his arm jutting away from his body, screaming in pain at The Creator, but his screams were stifled by the sound of thousands of tiny legs scraping on the stone ground. The man's head swivelled vigorously, trying to pinpoint where the danger was coming from. They came from all sides, heading straight for him. He could do nothing but beg The Creator for help, pleading for his life, crying for safety.

The insectoids converged on the man, immediately enveloping him. The Creator stood unmoved, curious to observe how they killed. Chunks of the man were thrown from the writhing pile of insectoids, his screams choked by the crushing bodies of the creatures. They dug into his soft flesh, scuttling into his body, tearing through his organs, and bursting back out. Blood flowed freely from his mouth, and his eyes quickly became dark with death, and once the insectoids had satisfied their hunger, they departed, leaving a pile of bones thinly cloaked with skin and flesh, and a skull which had retained parts of the man's face. Picking up the skull, The Creator turned it over in his hands, examining in detail the damage and taking in the carnage he had witnessed.

"Fascinating."

That was all he said before dropping the skull and turning his attention back to his creations. He saw that some of them were carrying chunks of the man away, and, confident that this would lead him to the insectoid queen, he followed in the wake of the creatures. They scuttled through the town, showing The Creator more scenes of carnage, homes with destroyed doors and windows painted red, more caved-in cars, and parts of people strewn across the paths and the roads. Eventually, the creatures moved into one of these destroyed homes, and entering, The Creator saw the home of the queen.

The creatures inhabited the bottom floor of the house. The floor and walls were covered with a thick slime of sludge, a mixture of coagulated blood, human viscera, and excretions from the insectoids. Walking through this, The Creator also spotted humans being used as incubators. What he presumed was the family who had previously inhabited the house were slumped against various walls, swollen and groaning in pain. He saw the father with a rippling chest, clearly close to birthing more of The Creator's creations, and the corpse of a younger human, burst open, their use fulfilled. The mother, though, sat swollen, but without any movement like the father had. The Creator stooped down in front of her, but his presence did not even cause the woman to open her eyes. He lifted her shirt to look at her swollen torso. He prodded it, testing its firmness and curious to see if it would elicit any response from the creatures inside of her. When no response was given, The Creator was confident that the creatures were in an early stage of development. Disconnecting a section of his armour, he brandished a small knife. This he slipped under the woman's ribs and carefully glided the blade across the underside of her ribs, from left to right, so that her organs fell onto the floor. In reaction, the woman meekly let out a whimper, then her final breath, and died, escaping The Creator's experiment. Sifting through her organs, he located her stomach and cut it open, emptying its contents onto the floor. Spotting his target, The Creator lifted out one of the many embryos that had filled the woman, and he lifted it into the light, examining it. Satisfied with his choice, he sliced off some flesh for the queen and wiped off the blade, reconnected it to his armour, and stood up, cradling the embryo in one of his arms.

Continuing through the house, he entered the kitchen, which was where he found the queen. She was curled into a ball but unfurled upon the arrival of the flesh from the woman and greedily fed, devouring it in a matter of seconds. The queen stretched across the kitchen, easily measuring six feet in length. Her legs were more pronounced than the others; the joints had a wicked point on them, extending slightly beyond the bend of the legs. The plates on her back seemed to be thicker and a slightly flatter shape than those of the other insectoids, differentiating her from her offspring. Overjoyed with the evolution of his original insectoid, The Creator stepped towards it, stretching out his free arm, beckoning for her. Recognising her creator, the insectoid scuttled forward and up The Creator's arm, coiling around it and resting her head on his shoulder. Now that he had what he had come for, The Creator retreated from the house, leaving the insectoids in peace, content that they would fulfil their purpose when the time came. He entered the darkness once more and returned to his laboratory.

He opened a container for the queen to enter, and obediently she did, crawling quickly into it, and curling herself up to fit. Once the queen had been contained, The Creator retrieved a cylindrical container that was filled with a thick liquid, and in this, he placed the embryo that he had taken. It floated down into the liquid and was suspended in the middle of it. Sealing this off, he placed it among other samples and returned his attention to the queen. Picking up the container, he moved it over to the table, which had the disfigured man on it, lying where The Creator had left him.

> "The time of your final test is here. I have retrieved the queen of another race of beings, which I started. Together, the both of you will command the insectoids to victory and help me reach my goal. To do this, though, you two must join into one. This I have already prepared you for. It will be painful, as all good

> things are, but once this is done, you will be ready to serve and ready to go forth and change the world for the better."

Saying this, The Creator opened the container and lifted the queen onto the disfigured man's torso. She immediately dived into the trench that The Creator had refined, filling it like a poisoned, gangrenous river, and she burrowed into and out of the man's burst blisters, her legs scrabbling against the disfigured man's flesh as she surged up his torso. The man twisted and groaned at the pain, straining against the nails that pinned him down, but did not try to stop the queen. She filled the vacant spaces in his torso and reached his head. She dived into one of his empty eyes, sinking into his skull, her legs stripping skin and flesh away from around his eye socket as she forced her way in. The queen wrapped herself around the man's brain, squeezing it, and her body slunk between it and the disfigured man's skull. When she had fully wrapped herself around his brain, she sunk her legs into it, and her mandibles swung down, sinking into his brain as well, joining the two into one as the man's thoughts shot up the mandibles and began to mix and intertwine with those of the insectoid queen.

The disfigured man lay panting, recovering from the ordeal, and The Creator stood silently, waiting for the two to settle into one being. Once they had settled, the disfigured man stopped panting and the queen stopped writhing and lay still. The Creator pulled out the nails that restrained the disfigured man, and helped him to sit up. He quickly started to question the man, eager to see if his creation had been a success.

> "It is over. You have done well, but tell me, do you hear them? Can you hear the voices of the insectoids, their desires, their cries for their missing queen?"

The disfigured man seemed to concentrate for a moment, listening carefully for them. To The Creator's delight, the man nodded, signalling that he could hear the insectoids.

"You are now their leader. You have merged with their queen and now possess the ability to command them. Soon, you will command them in our battle. You must go to them, gather them. You must then spread them across the country and lay in wait. My dogs will begin the attacks. You will support them. I will take you to them now."

Leading the disfigured man into the darkness, The Creator took him back to the house where he had found the queen. He watched as the insectoids scuttled around the man, recognising the queen and the man as their leaders. The insectoids parted as the man approached, following close on his heels. Content that this section of his army was complete and ready, The Creator stepped out of the house and back onto the empty street. Breathing heavily, The Creator was ready to prepare the final creations for his crusade.

»»»»»»»

"We found it dying. It called to us to restore it. It has been rejected, forgotten by the world, but it will give us power. We have saved it, nursing it back to its rightful place.

"Through many trials, we have found what it needs. The blood of the mother, flesh of the innocent, the sacrifice of the father. We built it a church, a place of safety, a place to feed."

The Creator stepped into a singed field, pierced with blackened and smouldering pyres adorned with the charred and disintegrating corpses of the cult's victims. Moonlight struggled through the clouds, shooting shards of light onto the pyres. The Creator stood unmoving, his head slowly tilting to the right in curiosity. His *Sanguinas Cani* had been placed across the country, but the way they had been received has differed for each one. They've been pets, scientific mysteries, but something to be worshipped? This amused him. They would serve their purpose, but they were not something to be worshipped. He strolled through the empty husks, making his way towards the altar building. As he got closer, the sound of chanting and singing began to seep into the field, further amusing The Creator.

When he reached the entrance to the building, the cold, damp mist of the night clung to him, droplets of water coating his metal armour. Craning his neck up, he scrutinised the high, curved roof and the detailed stonework and carvings on the doors in front of him, depicting the discovery of his creature and their 'discovery' of what it needed to eat to grow.

Pushing open the doors, splintering the wood and metal locks holding them shut, The Creator dragged the cult's attention away from their festivities, now focusing them on his glittering form. The singing cut off abruptly, like he had cut their throats simultaneously. He continued into the centre of the altar, stepping past bloody mops and buckets of stained water, and turned to the cult members who were following his movements, transfixed and silent.

"I am here for your 'deity'. Bring it to me."

A stunned silence was the only response that The Creator received. When he was sure that no one was going to answer him, The Creator tried once more.

"The creature, **my** Sanguinas Canis, that you found, was **given**. I must now take it. So, bring it to me. It is not yours. It was never yours. Bring it to me."

The cult members looked at each other, unsure what to do, murmuring, some with wide eyes, some with wrinkled and furrowed eyebrows. From the back of the room, a voice echoed out, strong and assured, finally giving The Creator an answer.

"And who are you to ask for our deity? You appear to be a creature yourself and, therefore, have no higher authority than what we protect. We found it dying. It called to us. If you are, like you say, its creator, then why cast it out? Why–"

As the cult leader was saying this, he made his way forward, through the crowd, and up onto the altar, so he stood directly in front of The Creator, tilting his head up, glaring into his featureless face.

"You are not its protectors. You are merely an incubator that I do not need to attend to. You provide warmth, food whilst it grows, and when it is mature, I can then take it. You are a means to an end. Not special. Show me where you keep it."

"No. We will not offer up our deity to you!"

"Wrong. You will not offer it up, but someone will."

The cult leader's breath caught in his throat, making his face contort in confusion. Forcing his air out, trying to clear his throat, he felt spittle coat his chin. Wiping it off, he saw blood, increasing his confusion. Looking down, he was met with the sight of The Creator's arm caving in his ribcage. The Creator removed his arm, dragging his spine with it. Shards of ribs fell to the floor as The Creator wiped his hand clean on the cultist's robe. The man stumbled back, staring horrified at his torn chest. As he died, he thought that his chest looked like his deity's face. His ribs curved out of his chest like teeth, his torn flesh became dysfunctional lips, his spine the curling and curving tongue. A faint smile poked at the corners of his lips as he collapsed dead, blood leaking from his mouth.

The Creator turned to the stunned cult and asked again for his creation. One man, Isaac, moved forward and knelt over the corpse of his leader, resting his forehead on his. He looked tearfully up to The Creator and, with a quivering finger, pointed to a set of metal doors positioned behind the altar. Striding over to them, The Creator wrenched the doors apart like he was tearing paper and stepped back, allowing the creature to pad its way into the light. It froze in front of the unexpected audience, but continued its pacing towards The Creator, circling him, teasing him with swipes from its curved claws. Finally, after seemingly becoming satisfied, it lay down in front of him and rested its head on its front paws.

The Creator knelt down to the creature and placed his right hand on its forehead. A soft glow emanated from his hand, sinking into the creature's head. The veins throughout the creature's body stood out and the vertebrae pushed against its skin. It drew away from The Creator's touch, its mouth opening to let out a scream, but its cheeks tore instead, allowing its jaw to open wider, showing new teeth pushing out of its gums, its pre-existing teeth growing larger, leaving it with a mutilated grin, promising only death.

> "You are complete, my child. You are no longer unaware; you can understand me now. Form ideas. Strategise. Kill. Go forth and hunt, be what you were made to be."

The Creator stood up, raising his arms, a low, dark laughter seeping from him. The cult had been standing transfixed, watching this take place, but upon the beginning of the evolution, they had started to slowly back away, fear beginning to rise within them. The *Sanguinas Canis* had turned, prowling slowly forward, its tongue lashing out at them. Suddenly, it pounced, grabbing the nearest cultist, holding her down with one of its paws, slowly tightening its grip, slicing into her chest. Without warning, the creature opened its mouth and locked its jaws around her head, biting off her face, and as it pulled away, her brain, which was caught in its teeth, was tugged out and spread itself over the remainder of her skull. The creature continued its rampage, carving through the panicking crowd, slicing through legs, preventing the cultists from leaving. Heads caved under the pressure of its steps, blood poured from between its teeth, pleasure raced through it, malevolence growing and filling its body.

The Creator stood, unmoving, revelling in the scene of carnage, impatient to unleash his creations on the world. His trance was only broken when his creature left the cult as a sea of blood, diced and minced into something that could never be recognised as human. The Creator left the building, stepping into the quiet, misty night. The creature followed him out, standing beside him. The Creator pointed into the night, commanding it to go forth, kill, cause chaos, and start The Creator's remoulding of the world.

As he stood alone, anticipation rose within The Creator. Turning to face the cult's building, he raised his hands, making flames leap up the walls. They climbed to the peak of the curved roof and kept rising, climbing into the sky, forming a pillar of fire. His signals had been sent. He had released the dogs. No one knew it yet, but it had begun. The Creator was ready.

...AND AFTER

It began with just stories.

FAMILY OF FOUR MISSING

A family of four went missing late last night, according to local police.

The Jarrett family, 42-year-old William, his 40-year-old wife Heather, and their 13-year-old twin sons Jack and Alfie were reported missing by a relative. It appears that they disappeared from their home last night. Their door was found broken down, and the interior was a mess. The police also found a large amount of blood at the scene, causing concerns for the family's safety to grow.

MISSING HIKER FOUND DEAD

A BEAR ATTACK HAS CLAIMED THE LIVES OF AT LEAST 6 PEOPLE

Across the country, stories like these appeared simultaneously, leaving us no time to put the pieces together or realise what was happening, but this is how it all began. Hundreds of these stories, hundreds of dead, but people only became suspicious on the day of the sieges. The targets were the major cities of the US states that the dogs had been placed in, systematically taking down any areas that could house significant resistance.

THE SIEGES

Every siege went differently; the following section is the account of the siege in Virginia.

The city was given at least some warning before its death. The dog entered the city as a wave of death, killing anyone it could catch. It took its time, tearing off the roofs of cars to decapitate the cowering inhabitants, bursting through building walls, herding everyone forward, sending hordes of terrified people running for their lives deeper into the city. The dog would swipe at those falling behind, stripping the flesh from their backs. In some cases, its claws would hook onto the spines and tear them out, like de-boning a fish.

All the chaos and noise led to the police to barricade the city centre, lining it with cars for cover and waves of heavily armed officers, hellbent on killing the creature. The horde of people reached the centre, swarming past the police, leaving the creature standing alone, staring at the arsenal it faced.

The first shot was fired, grazing the creature, a spray of black blood flying in the air. A symphony of gunshots followed, driving the thing back and leaving it licking its wounds behind a deserted bus. Within this bus, though, sat a woman, curled into a ball in the creature's shadow. It noticed her, but instead of killing her, it tore a hole in the side of the bus and retreated slightly, allowing the woman to run to the police line.

As soon as the officers lowered their guns to allow the woman to pass through them, the creature bounded forward, landing on the roof of one of the police vehicles, and began tearing into the line. In one swipe, three officers fell to the ground headless, the creature moving on before their bodies hit the ground. It bit into the arm of another, placing a paw on his chest to hold him still and tearing off the limb, leaving the man writhing on the ground, his left hand trying to cover the stump of his right arm.

As the massacre continued, news and police helicopters began to circle overhead, like vultures over a freshly killed gazelle. The police inside the helicopters opened fire, sending down bullets like lethal hail onto the creature, tearing through its flesh. It stopped its massacre to turn and find the helicopters, lashing its tongue at them with searing hatred. It picked up a policeman who was crawling, bleeding, away from it and launched the man at the helicopters, sending him crashing into the side of one of them, smashing open his head like an egg, but not bringing down the vehicle. This time, the creature stripped off the roof of a car and threw that, sending it spinning through the helicopter's cockpit, slicing through the pilots. The helicopter began to dive and spin widely, clipping the other helicopters, police tumbling out of its open doors, falling screaming into the city. The helicopters collided with buildings, sending down a storm of broken glass and landing in a fireball at the bottom, transferring the fire to them. Turning back to the police line, the creature resumed its assault, only now the hail of bullets had left it bleeding, inspiring them with new hope. They continued to attack, aiming for the creature's joints, hoping to immobilise it. One shot finally broke through the dog's unusually hard bone and sent shards of its knee scattering onto the sidewalk.

The creature screeched in pain, fracturing the windows in the cars, its back end collapsing, giving the police enough time to move towards it and increase the accuracy of their shots. Soon, another limb was felled, and the creature was now lying on the ground, one arm left, swiping pointlessly at the police who stood out of its reach, and its tongue whipping hungrily at the air. The police continued to shoot at the shoulder of the final arm, not stopping until it lay disconnected from the body, strings of muscle and skin moving gently in the wind, covered in the *Sanguinas'* blood, which was leaking from its many injuries and forming a lake of unearthly blood.

Moving up the creature, the police levelled the barrels of their weapons at its head and, without hesitation, proceeded to empty them into it, cracking the skull and turning the head black with blood. To finish it, the police proceeded to stamp down on its head, first caving it in, warping the creature's cruel smile, and then flattening it, leaving it nothing more than chunks of flesh and bone floating in its own blood. Cheers resounded through the city, relief replacing terror. Unbeknownst to them, the insectoids were stirring in the sewer system, surging towards manhole covers and exits to the city.

The insectoid outbreak began in the centre of the US. From there, the insectoids spread out in contingents into every state. They waited under the capital cities, and when the Sanguinas Cani were killed, they entered the city, which now had its defences weakened and a large portion of the population in one place, so the insectoids could quickly increase their numbers.

The police had turned away from the corpse and were starting to try and establish some semblance of control. The manhole covers began to rattle and then shot off, unleashing a tsunami of black death. The police spun but were overcome, coated, and sliced to ribbons under the insectoids' razor legs. The crowd scattered, followed closely by the insectoids. The corpse of the *Sanguinas Canis* was dragged into the centre of the square by the bugs, and its body began to combust, exploding into a pillar of fire. Out of this fire flew more of The Creator's creatures:

Mors Volans – Winged creatures that had no legs or head. Their bodies were oval-shaped, and the chest was formed of a circular mouth. This mouth was lined with layers and layers of sharp teeth whose edges were serrated like a saw's blade, so they could cut through any material they met. The teeth also oscillated in the gums, adding more force to the creature's attack, so that a minor injury was not possible – a glancing blow and the creature would chew to

THE RIOTING OF INFERNO

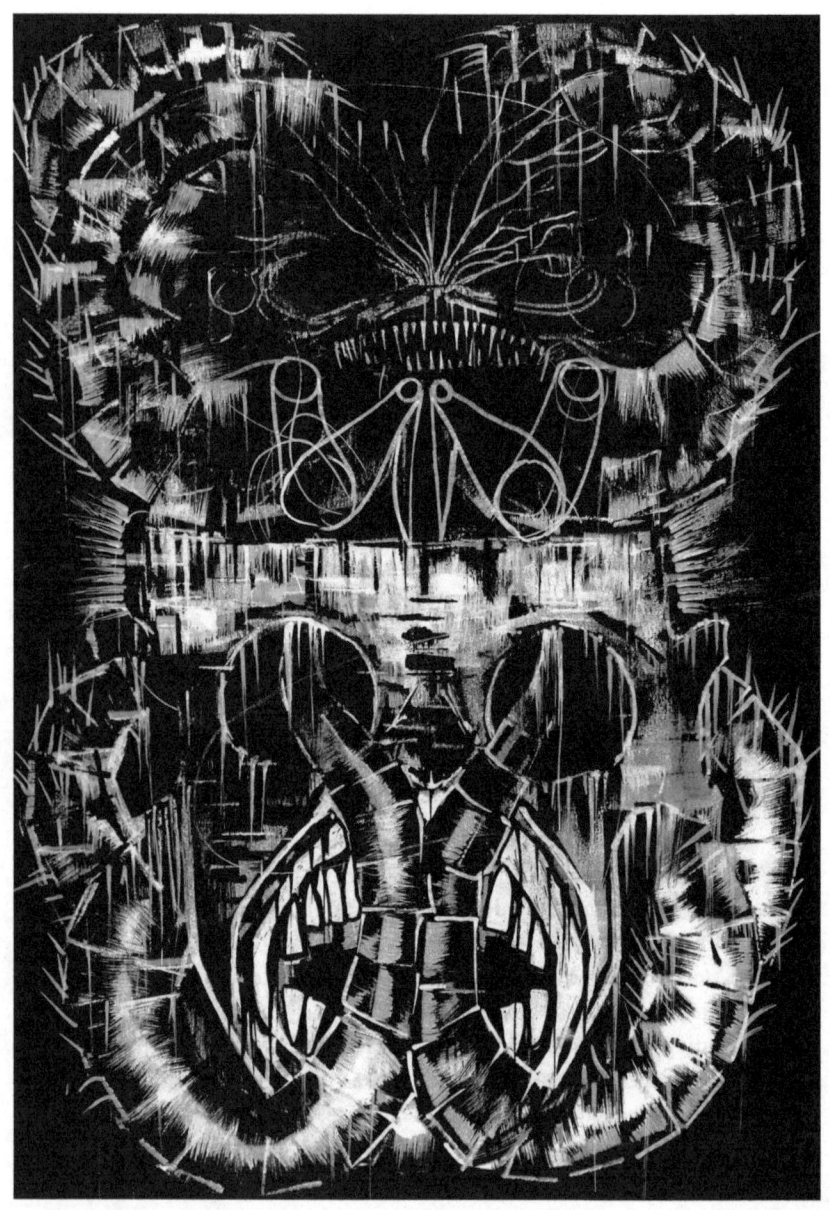

the bone or destroy the jugular. Their wings were jointed, allowing them to walk if they were on the ground, and ended in a pincer-like claw, giving them the ability to hold objects or grip their prey.

Mortem Amplexers - Quadrupedal creatures, shorter than the *Sanguinas Cani*. They had round bodies, twice the size of a desktop globe, covered with what appeared to be jet-black fur. Each hair, though, had the strength of metal, and acted as a sharp needle, and as there were so many of them, one hit left its prey with hundreds of small punctures, which caused internal bleeding. The hairs were also hollow and injected a poison, which first attacked the muscles, breaking down the cells and paralysing the prey. This poison then went on to dissolve the organs, and the prey died by drowning on their dissolved lungs. This left the prey's skin acting as a sack or a bottle, holding the liquid organs, flesh and bones. The *Mortem Amplexer* then returned and punctured the corpse again, but, this time, the hair acted as a straw, and the creature fed through drinking the liquidised insides. Their arms and legs were long and folded under the body. Their pale-yellow skin stretched tightly over rippling muscles. The fingers and toes were thin and long, with three joints, and these allowed both the feet and the hands to be able to grip and hold objects. Its head was featureless, only marked with two fleshy holes, which were its ears.

Like the other states, Virginia had fallen. A gateway to The Creator's home had been opened, and the insectoids killed the inhabitants in hours.

This was how the country fell. Every state was attacked simultaneously, taking out the possibility that people could be warned of what was coming. By 4.00pm, the day after The Creator released the final *Sanguinas Canis*, everywhere but the US capital had been destroyed. The last story to come out of America, before it was completely lost and the rest of the world began to prepare for their own assaults, was the battle for the White House. It represented the last stronghold of humanity in the country; its fences were fortified and guards filled the fields around the building. This was where The Creator revealed himself.

He stood in front of the gate to the property, and behind him stood his army. His *Mors Volans* hovered above him, forming clouds of death, and waves upon waves of *Mortem Amplexers* shuddered with anticipation. Underground, creatures that looked like armoured drills, with spines that could shoot through the earth *(Spina Curniculos)* and a creature that could unsettle the dirt, liquifying it and making its target fall into its mouth *(Contra Laqueums)*, lay in wait, their presence unknown by the army.

> "Let us in. I have taken your country, killed your people. There is no reason to resist us now. If you resist, the only thing I can promise is a painful death. You no longer own this land."

The Creator was interrupted by planes overhead, firing into the horrific crowd. The *Mors Volans* immediately took to the offensive, flying directly to the planes. Some flew straight into their engines, causing the planes to explode, sending debris raining onto both forces, but only the humans dived for cover. Some of the *Mors Volans* landed on the cockpit windows and, with their toothed undersides, drilled through the polycarbonate windows and fell onto the pilots, blitzing their torsos into a red mist.

The Creator watched this silently and sent his forces forward, taking the fight above them as a sign that the humans would not surrender. The army fired through the gates, creating walls of bullets. The bullets shattered and deflected off the hides of the *Mortem Amplexers*. The creatures had leapt forward, but the barrage made them pause and step back, unsure of their own safety. After a few seconds, they realised that they were not being harmed by the human weapons and continued forward, climbing over the gates and dropping smoothly onto the grass. They bounded towards the soldiers, and when they got close, they pounced, arms and legs outstretched, and landed heavily on them, the hairs easily sinking through the armour, their limbs wrapping around and squeezing the soldiers further onto the hairs, maximising the poison's dose. When satisfied, the creatures pushed off the felled soldiers, eliciting pained grunts, and then moved on to their next victims. The attacked soldiers tried to climb to their feet, but their limbs could only twitch, and soon they began to howl, their organs dissolving, and blood leaked from their mouths, ears, eyes, and nose, becoming less human, losing humanity, becoming sacks of food.

Behind them, the remaining lines started to fire on the front line, not caring about whether the soldiers were still alive, hoping to overwhelm the things with their firepower. Underneath them, the subterranean creatures had positioned themselves under the soldiers, and spines, shot with high pressure, burst through the dirt and sailed through the soldiers' bodies, pinning them in place. The spikes were bone-white, making the blood of the soldiers stand out as it dribbled down and stained the spikes. The soldiers were screaming in pain; their deaths would come after hours of slow bleeding, their bones broken, and limbs twisted from the force carried by the spines. The *Contra Laqueums* then began to liquefy the soil behind the retreating army, creating spots of quicksand-like dirt. Soldiers fell unexpectedly into it, sinking immediately to their knees. They began to panic as they sank, and their shouts for help became shouts of pain as their legs reached the creature's mouths, which began to bite down and pull them apart. Their torsos burst under the creature's bite, fertilising the soil with blood, and their heads were left above ground, their dull eyes staring unblinkingly at the chaos and death which surrounded them.

Walking through the bloody, chaotic battle, The Creator approached the White House, breaking down its doors, and entered. He moved through it systematically; any inhabitants he found perished under his power. With ease, he would tear anyone who fought against him in half. Those who tried to worship him, he would step on their heads, cracking them under the pressure. Rooms became strewn with body parts, carpets soaked with brain matter, the gurgle of blood filling the silence The Creator had made. A pillar of fire grew from the building's roof, signifying the end of the human resistance and the arrival of more creatures.

The Creator stood staring out the window onto the lawn,

watching the death and his creatures flourish. Out of the darkness, he summoned the leader of the insectoids, the *Impii Matrim*. Stepping out of the darkness, it stood in front of The Creator, the insectoid queen moving and writhing through him.

"Have the insectoid numbers grown?"

"Yes, the cities provided enough flesh to triple our numbers. At your command, we are ready to expand out of the country."

"Good. Spread until you reach the oceans. Spread fear. Spread death."

Silently, the *Impii Matrim* returned to the darkness, and to its forces, ready to lead them into untouched territory. Turning back to the window, The Creator watched contently the feast in which his creatures were indulging.

The White House was surrounded by corpses, bloated skin sacks being sucked dry by *Mortem Amplexers*, the twitching, pinned victims moaning quietly. *Mors Volans* descended on the heads of the buried victims of the *Contra Laqueums*, their claws sinking into their temples, and their teeth drilling through the top of the skulls, sucking up the dead brains. The sky had now turned a sulphuric orange, the screeches and calls of creatures had now replaced the hum of people and cars, and The Creator prepared to expand his rule.

Within twenty-four hours of the fall of North America, contact was lost with the rest of the Americas. As of now, contact has been lost with another twenty-three countries, and it is clear that Asia is being lost. Accounts of amphibian creatures have been sent from the coast of Italy, so we will not be safe for long. It is obvious that this will be our extinction.

This is our end.

Love Your Book

The Rioting of Inferno

TIMELINE

MARCH 2024

Soft-back book printed from paper that has been carbon offset through the World Land Trust Scheme.

PRINTED by Hobbs the Printers Ltd
at Southampton, United Kingdom

PUBLISHED by Cybirdy Publishing
London, United Kingdom

SPECIAL EDITION
Autographed by the Author

E.J. COUSINS

WHO are you?	WHO did you obtain the book from?	WHEN did you obtain the book
FIRST GUARDIAN		
SECOND GUARDIAN		
THIRD GUARDIAN		
FOURTH GUARDIAN		
FIFTH GUARDIAN		

E.J. Cousins, 17, (Hertfordshire, England), loves the disgusting. He is an avid fan of cinema, especially horror. Influenced by the work of David Cronenberg, Quentin Tarantino, and Dario Argento, he has become fascinated with the connection between beautiful images and disgusting actions. This influence spreads further to literature, principally Edgar Allen Poe and H.G. Wells with their blending of science fiction and psychological horror. Ethan has been writing short horror stories since the age of 14, and with this first book, he follows in the footsteps of these great film makers and writers, who love the disgusting.